Beyond the North Wind

by Gillian Bradshaw

Greenwillow Books, New York

Printed in the United States of America

First Edition   10 9 8 7 6 5 4 3 2 1

Library of Congress Cataloging-in-Publication Data

Bradshaw, Gillian (date)
   Beyond the north wind / by Gillian Bradshaw.
      p.   cm.
Summary: The Greek god Apollo sends a talented
young magician on a quest to stop an evil queen
from exterminating a small tribe of griffins.
   ISBN 0-688-11357-5
   [1. Fantasy.]   I. Title.
PZ7.B7277Be   1993
[Fic]—dc20   92-9671   CIP   AC

For Sara,
who liked the other ones

Contents

. . . beyond the Issedones live the one-eyed
Arimaspians, and beyond them the griffins which
guard the gold, and beyond the griffins the Hyperboreans—
the people beyond the North Wind. . . .

HERODOTUS, *Histories,* Book IV, Chapter 13,
referring to the information in
a lost poem by Aristeas of Proconnesus

The Arimaspians

1

They'd told Aristeas that the Arimaspians were horrible, but he wasn't prepared for how horrible they were, and it nearly cost him his life.

He was huddled over his campfire that cold spring night, plunking a mournful little tune on his lyre, when his horse gave a sudden neigh of terror, and a shape loomed out of the darkness on the other side of the fire and stood motionless in the red light, grinning. Aristeas dropped the lyre and stared.

The man facing him was huge; his head towered up into the night like smoke, and he was dressed in loose skins that made him seem even bigger. He held a long black stick, wrapped in leather, its end in one hand. His hair was red and bristled, and his teeth were too big; they hung out over his lower lip, sharp and yellow. But the worst thing about him was his eye. It was when he saw the eye that Aristeas realized this was an Arimaspian; he'd been told that Arimaspians had only one eye. But he'd always thought that meant one *normal* eye where an eye should be. The Arimaspian's eye was on the bridge of his nose, and it was a red hole with a glare inside like fire. Where

1

his eyes should have been were two slight hollows covered by smooth skin, like the soft spot on a baby's skull. The blankness where the eyes should have been, and the glare where it shouldn't be, were unexpectedly sickening.

Aristeas was so shocked that he couldn't think of anything to do. He didn't reach for his bowcase to defend himself or jump onto his horse and try to escape. He just sat, staring in horror. His horse recovered more quickly: It reared, neighing again, then galloped off into the night. Then there was a step behind him, something crashed onto the back of his head, and everything was gone.

He woke in complete blackness. He was far too numb to feel anything, even pain or fear. His own arms and legs seemed wooden, as though they didn't belong to him, and he couldn't move. He could see nothing, but he could hear voices speaking nearby.

"Colaxis will be angry," one was saying. It was a deep, croaking voice, like a bullfrog. "You shouldn't have hit so hard."

"She can't blame me because it died!" answered another voice. It was a bit higher, like a smaller frog. "I had to hit it; it would have got its bow out otherwise and shot both of us. Here's the bow, look! It's not my fault it died from a little tap on the head."

"Skylas, calling that blow a little tap is like calling a pine tree a tallish piece of grass! You meant to kill the creature. And you know that Colaxis wants any humans her scouts catch. It's been a month since she had a bite of human flesh, and you know it's her favorite dish. If she finds out that we caught a human and ate it ourselves, she'll have our hides for carpets."

"Colaxis is a greedy sow!" Skylas said in an angry whine. "I like the taste of humans myself, Hyrgis, and so do you. If we had kept this one for Colaxis, we'd have been lucky to get a shinbone each to gnaw on. Come on, look at this one!" Aristeas felt something through the numbness, a hand prodding him. He began to feel just a little bit afraid, too. "Nice lean meat," Skylas said, pinching. "I hate too much fat on a human, don't you? It's so greasy. But this one's not too thin either. I'll bet it has a big, juicy liver, all crumbly and delicious! Don't you want to get your teeth into it? We can dry the leftovers when we've finished and bring Colaxis those."

"She likes fresh meat," croaked Hyrgis. "Her orders were quite clear: Any humans captured by her scouts are to be brought to her alive and with all their gear. And I think she would have particularly wanted to question this creature first. There's something very strange about it. What was it doing here in our territory all alone? It doesn't have any herds it was pasturing."

"It probably was running away from some human enemy and thought our people were still at the winter campsites down south."

"I don't know," said Hyrgis doubtfully. "Look at what it had in its saddlebags! Have you ever seen anything like this?"

Skylas was silent; over the crackle of the fire Aristeas heard the rustle of parchment and knew they'd found his book of poems and his map.

"It's some kind of leather," Skylas said after a minute. He sounded a bit frightened now. "But what are all those markings on it? Do you suppose they're magic?"

"How would I know? But if it is, Colaxis will want to know all about it, and who's going to tell her, with the human dead? And another thing, this human isn't dressed like any human I've ever seen before. It's foreign, not from any of the nearby tribes. Forget your stomach for a moment, and look at its clothes, for a change!" A hand pulled at Aristeas again, and when it turned him over, he realized he'd been lying facedown on the earth, because as he turned, the blackness changed back into firelight. The numbness was replaced by a blinding pain in his head. Someone gave a whimper of pain, and when the hand jerked away, Aristeas realized it had been he.

"It's alive!" exclaimed Hyrgis.

"Uh?" Skylas said in astonishment. "I was sure I'd killed it!"

Aristeas blinked, cleared his eyes, and saw two Arimaspians looking down at him with their red eyeholes. He closed his eyes quickly.

There was another silence; then Skylas said slyly, "It still might die after that kind of knock on the head. We ought to question it ourselves, and then maybe . . . finish it off, and, yummmm—"

"No!" said Hyrgis firmly. "Colaxis might have forgiven us for killing it accidentally when we caught it, but she'd never excuse us for killing it now."

"Who'd tell her?" asked Skylas.

"She'd find out," Hyrgis said. "Do you think she can't use her magic powers on you? She can and she will, and unless you know how to fight magic, you ought to treat the property of powerful witches with respect. Stop poking the human. Colaxis will be pleased with us when we give it to her. Until then we'll have to keep it alive and safe."

Skylas snarled. "Dried horsemeat for supper again, when we have a nice fresh human lying there! I'm sick of dried horsemeat! Why didn't you catch the human's horse? Then at least we could have had fresh horsemeat!"

"Even if I had caught the human's horse, we couldn't

have eaten it. We would have had to keep it to carry the human. As it is, thanks to you and your 'little tap,' we're going to have to do the carrying ourselves. Seven days' walk, and in mountainous country, too! Eight days, more likely, if we have to carry it all the way. Though maybe it'll be able to walk in a few days. Human! Do you hear me?"

Reluctantly Aristeas opened his eyes again. He looked up at the bristle-haired glare-eyed face above him and groaned.

Hyrgis grinned, showing all his too-big yellow teeth. "You do hear me! Good. Can you move?"

He couldn't, and it was too much effort to say so. He closed his eyes and groaned again.

"Limp as a skinned squirrel," Hyrgis observed to Skylas. "But we'd better tie him up, all the same. Go fetch the rope."

Skylas fetched a leather rope, and the two Arimaspians began tying Aristeas's hands and feet. He didn't try to stop them. Hyrgis noticed the knife Aristeas wore on his belt, drew it, admired it, and fastened it to his own belt instead, and still, Aristeas didn't resist. The numbness was all gone now, and he felt awful: sick and dizzy with a pounding headache. They can't fight magic, he told himself. They as good as said they can't. And magic is something I'm good at. So I have a chance to get away . . . when I'm feeling better.

But he knew he had to escape before the two Arimaspians brought him to this Colaxis, this ruler of theirs who was a witch. Seven or eight days, they'd said. He had to be able to walk—no, run!—before then. He'd certainly need magic to do that.

The Arimaspians brought a horsehide and rolled it around Aristeas, then put his own blanket over the top.

"Are you warm enough?" asked Hyrgis, tucking it in.

Aristeas didn't answer. He felt too miserable.

"You'll stay alive for a little while yet," Hyrgis told him, "and we'll look after you. Don't struggle. You'd only hurt yourself. You can't escape."

Aristeas said nothing. Hyrgis and Skylas went over to the fire and began eating some of the detested dried horsemeat, chewing it noisily. Skylas kept screwing up his face and looking regretfully at Aristeas. Aristeas closed his eyes so he wouldn't see, because the sight of the Arimaspian's yellow teeth chomping and dribbling the dried meat made him feel even more sick. He struggled to concentrate and tried to shape a piece of music in his mind. It wouldn't come right. He set his teeth and tried again, tried until he was sweating with tension, and in the end he felt the tune wobble into place. The throbbing of his head faded a little—but only a little. Then he lost the shape of the tune again, and he was too exhausted to try once more. Being knocked on the head had affected his ability to work magic as much as his ability to do anything else. He lay limply, feeling the tears of exhaustion, pain, and self-pity welling from his eyes. Give it a few days, he told himself, trying to cheer himself up. You'll feel better in the morning; try again then.

He did feel a little better in the morning—but again, not very much. The Arimaspians fetched some water and boiled it in Aristeas's own copper pot, then washed the back of Aristeas's head and bandaged it with a strip of deerhide. The amount of blood that came out of his hair when they washed the injury, and the way it made him dizzy, frightened him. He was obviously badly hurt. Probably some bones in his skull had cracked. How could he escape in this condition? He *had* to work that spell to heal himself.

At least in the sunlight the Arimaspians didn't look

quite as huge and terrifying as they had in the firelight the night before. Aristeas guessed that the top of his head would reach about to the level of Skylas's shoulder. Skylas was shorter and fatter than Hyrgis, and his bristly hair was a dirty yellow color. He still looked very sulky about not being allowed to eat the prisoner, particularly when some more dried horsemeat appeared for breakfast. Hyrgis, however, slouched over to Aristeas and offered him a piece of the meat.

Aristeas looked at the stringy strip, black from smoking and stiff as old leather. He shuddered and closed his eyes, and Hyrgis shrugged and slouched away again.

The two Arimaspians might not be as tall as giants, but they were certainly very strong. When they'd finished eating, they chopped down two saplings that were growing nearby with a few blows of a stone ax. They made a stretcher with these and the horsehide, put Aristeas on it, and strapped him in. Each of them picked up a heavy pack with his own supplies, and then Hyrgis slung Aristeas's own saddlebags over his shoulders as though they weighed nothing at all. Skylas picked up Aristeas's bowcase. He took the bow out and, after a few tries, succeeded in stringing it. "I've always wanted one of these," he said.

"It will only break," said Hyrgis, "but take it if you want it." He bent over and picked up the lyre, which was lying where Aristeas had dropped it the night before. For the first time since he was hit on the head, Aristeas found himself fully awake and angry. There was his beautiful lyre, with its lovely curved frame of polished wood and its tortoiseshell sounding board, clutched in the Arimaspian's huge, grimy hand. Hyrgis turned it upside down, shook it, then, with an air of reluctance, shoved it neckfirst into Aristeas's saddlebags. "Colaxis might want to see it," he explained. He picked up the front of the stretcher. "Come on!"

The Arimaspians began walking eastward with great strides, going quickly through an area of light woodland and scrub. Aristeas lay very still, trying to make himself numb again; the swaying of the stretcher jarred his head and hurt horribly. After a while he closed his eyes and tried to concentrate again on music. Music to ease the pain and to join together the cracked bones of his head. Lots of beautiful music. He struggled with it, fell asleep, then woke up and struggled some more. After a time it became easier to concentrate, and he realized that this was because his head wasn't hurting so much. The spell was working. It was pitifully hard, though. Compared with the way he usually felt when he worked magic, it was as though he were crawling on his hands and knees in a thick fog. But he kept on trying, and the more he concentrated, the easier it became. When the Arimaspians stopped at noon, he was still too weak to move. But when they made camp that evening, he felt much stronger and was starting to feel hungry. When Hyrgis offered him some more dried horsemeat, however, he shuddered again.

"You must eat," said Hyrgis sternly. "You'll become sick if you don't."

"I certainly will be sick if I eat that," answered Aristeas. "Don't you have anything else?"

Hyrgis didn't. He thought for a minute, then said, "I know, I'll boil some of this up for you and you can have the broth."

Aristeas was going to refuse that as well when he realized that he would need to eat to recover his strength. "Put some herbs in it then," he said.

"Some what?" asked Hyrgis in surprise.

"Well, some of that wild thyme over there, for a start,

and maybe a couple of roots from that meadowsweet, over there. And season it with salt and pepper—I've got some in my saddlebags."

"Do you think I'm a cook?" demanded Hyrgis indignantly.

"No, but I don't think I can drink boiled dried horsemeat soup plain. I'd be sick, and then, as you pointed out, I'd become ill. In fact, with a head injury like mine, I might die on the spot. Your friend Skylas would like that, but Colaxis wouldn't."

"What do you know about Colaxis?" Hyrgis asked suspiciously.

"Nothing. Just that you want me to be alive when you reach her. You said so last night."

Hyrgis looked a bit confused but apparently decided that he'd better do as he'd been asked. In the end, the meat broth actually smelled quite tasty, and Aristeas sat up, very cautiously, to drink it. His hands had been tied in front of him, so he could hold the bowl. Skylas picked up the cooking pot while Hyrgis was giving the prisoner the soup. He sniffed it, then poured the remains down his throat, and chomped on the sludgy meat at the bottom. But besides the boiled meat, there were half a dozen black peppercorns, and when Skylas crunched them, he gave out a bloodcurdling yell.

"Ow, ow, ow!" he shouted, jumping up and down. "Ow! The black seeds are made of fire!"

Aristeas laughed, and his head hurt again.

"Don't you laugh!" wailed Skylas. "You've poisoned me, you miserable human!"

"Pepper isn't a poison," Aristeas told him. "It's just a hot spice. You shouldn't eat it except ground up. I wanted some in my soup because I don't like the taste of dried horsemeat any more than you do."

Skylas just howled and ran off to get a drink of water.

Hyrgis squinted at Aristeas. His forehead crinkled up when he squinted, just like an ordinary man's, but his eyehole narrowed so that the glare in it shone brighter. "Feeling better this evening, are you, human?" he asked. "Then maybe you can answer a few questions. Where are you from?"

Aristeas was quiet for a moment. He did not like telling lies. But there was no reason not to answer truthfully. "I'm a Greek," he said.

Hyrgis stared with his horrible red eye. "I've never heard of this Greek tribe," he said suspiciously. "Where do your people live?"

"A very long way to the west and a long way south."

"A long way? How many days' journey?"

Aristeas sighed. "Two years'. Riding. But I stopped in the winters."

Hyrgis gave an impressed kind of grunt. "Where did you learn our language then? And why were you camping in the land of the Arimaspians?"

Skylas came back, still sniffing from the pepper, and crouched down beside Hyrgis, glaring at Aristeas. "Are you asking him if he's a magician?" he demanded.

"I wanted to learn about your people," Aristeas said quickly, so he wouldn't have to answer that question. "You see, I came east before, some years ago. But that time I wandered everywhere on the way and only got as far east as the lands of the Issedones, your human neighbors to the west. I spent some time with them and learned the northern language there. They told me stories about Arimaspians. After I'd visited the Issedones, I went home again, and I composed a poem about my journey. I called it 'Arimaspea—Tales of the Arimaspians.' This was all true, and he realized with pleasure that he could flatter the Arimaspians a bit and maybe put them off their guard. "The poem was a great success in my home city, Proconnesus. Everyone who heard it was fascinated by what I said about your people—but after I'd been home about a month, people started telling me that they didn't believe it. They said that the Issedones must have been telling me lies, and that there were no Arimaspians, and none of the griffins who fight you in the stories, and no Hyperboreans to the north of you.

"Well, there are no Arimaspians in Proconnesus or anywhere else where Greeks live. Anyway, I've come back east. I thought I could at least discover the truth of the stories." He had to be careful here. What he'd said was true, but it wasn't the real reason he'd made the long journey east again. He decided to try more flattery. "I thought that when I'd seen you myself and witnessed your magnificence, I could go home again and compose another poem that would silence all the disbelievers. I can carry your fame to the ends of the earth—uh, if I get home again, that is."

"What's a poem?" asked Skylas.

"It's a kind of song," answered Hyrgis before Aristeas could say anything. "Humans like them."

"I hate music!" Skylas said savagely.

"Of course," Hyrgis told him calmly. "We all hate music. It's in our natures." He squinted at Aristeas again. "Do you mean, you came all that way, and walked straight into our territory, so that you could compose a song?"

"Um . . . well, I hoped to compose one. And, uh, I'm not just a poet. I'm a servant of the god my people call Apollo. I don't know what you call him, but he's the god of light and of healing, and of music and poetry, the archer god, who killed the earth serpent. I, uh, hoped that however fierce you were to your enemies, you'd treat me with kindness because I served such a great god."

There was a moment of silence, and then both Arimaspians burst out laughing.

"You thought we wouldn't hurt you because we were afraid of this god?" asked Skylas. "We don't care a thing for the gods! We're not weak and fearful like humans! We're strong!"

"You shouldn't say anything like that!" said Aristeas, genuinely shocked. "The gods don't like it!"

"We don't care!" said Skylas. "Let them sulk in the heavens till they're black in the face."

"Do you know why we have only one eye?" asked Hyrgis, smiling unpleasantly.

"No," whispered Aristeas.

"Our ancestors were human and had two eyes," said Hyrgis. "But long ago one of them, a very powerful witch, got tired of human life. Human life is always full of tears. People die, things are lost, and when there's nothing else to cry about, humans listen to music and songs, to remind themselves how sad everything is, and cry over those. So our ancestress worked a great spell on her own family. She closed up their eyes so that they would never shed tears again, and she opened another eye into their heads, so that they could see clearly. And since then our people have grown stronger and stronger. We kill the humans we meet and eat them as though they were animals, and we're afraid of nothing, not even the gods."

"We hate everything weak," put in Skylas. "I'd kill you for making stupid songs about us, even if I weren't hungry." He glared at Aristeas again.

Aristeas swallowed. He'd hoped they might treat him more kindly. He hadn't really expected it, but he'd hoped.

"But the Issedones say," he told the two, daringly, "that however strong your people are, they're stupid. They say that you can't make bows, and don't know how to shoot, and that even when you steal a bow from a human, you break it. You can't tame horses and make them carry you, and you can't spin and weave cloth or forge metal. And because of that, the Issedones say they aren't afraid of you."

Skylas raised his hand to hit Aristeas, but Hyrgis stopped him. "He's for Colaxis," the bigger Arimaspian reminded his friend, and Skylas sat back, glaring. Hyrgis, however, smiled at Aristeas.

"It's true that the Issedones and the other human tribes have learned all sorts of things we haven't. They can make bows and forge metal into swords and spears, and they can tame horses and dogs to help them hunt. But soon we'll have all those secrets as well as our own strength. We have a queen now who's a witch as powerful as our great ancestress, and she'll soon find ways to defeat all our enemies. Already she's given her guards magical bows that don't break, and she's taming horses to carry them. Soon we'll be able to ride to war with the Issedones, and since we're stronger than they are, we'll defeat them. Then they'll be our slaves, and we'll feast on them whenever we like."

Skylas licked his lips, nodding.

Aristeas stared in horror. He had friends among the Issedones. And if the Arimaspians could conquer the Issedones, would they stop at that? "Ah . . . this queen . . ." he began.

"Colaxis," said Skylas with satisfaction.

". . . how long has she been your ruler?" Aristeas finished nervously.

"Nine years," answered Hyrgis, also with satisfaction.

"One spring nine years ago she murdered her parents and her enemies, and she's been our only ruler since."

"It—it wouldn't have been in early spring, would it?" asked Aristeas. "In the first month of spring, about the middle of the month, and around noon?"

The Arimaspians looked at him in surprise and suspicion. "Yes," said Hyrgis. "How did you know that? Are you a magician, human?"

Aristeas swallowed again. "I had . . . an omen given to me at that time," he said. It was true. Nine years ago he'd first had the feeling that there was a terrible danger in the east, a catastrophe that he was somehow expected to prevent. He'd traveled as far as the Issedones, trying to discover what the danger was, but he was sick of wandering by the time he reached them, and there was no sign of any terrible threat. So he'd done what he really wanted to do and gone home. But the sense of danger had just grown stronger and stronger, and in the end he'd had to come back. Now, at last, he understood what the danger was.

O Apollo, he thought miserably, how am I supposed to do anything about it? Especially with a cracked skull! O Apollo, I'd be so happy if you'd let me stay in Proconnesus! I'd be married by now. I might even have children. I'd help on the farm, I'd enter poems in the city competitions, and maybe even in the big competitions with other cities, and everyone would congratulate me when I won—it would be such a good life! And instead here I am at the end of the world, wounded, tied hand and foot, and on my way to a horrible Arimaspian witch who'll question me first, and then eat me. O Apollo, I wish, I wish, I *wish* you'd left me alone!

Griffins
2

When Aristeas woke the next morning, he at once felt happier. It was as though he'd gone to sleep with everything covered by a heavy fog and woken to find the sun shining. He couldn't have said how he knew, but he was sure that his magic was almost back to normal. He concentrated on the healing music again, and immediately the last of the headache faded and vanished away. He grinned, then hummed a different tune under his breath, a loosening, relaxing sort of tune. After a minute the ropes around his wrists and ankles had stretched so that he could slip them off whenever he liked, and he stopped. It wouldn't do to let the Arimaspians know he could get free. The best thing to do, he decided, would be to pretend he was still very ill and completely helpless; that way his captors wouldn't do anything that made it harder for him to escape. So when Hyrgis came to see how he was, he groaned pitifully and sipped the meat broth he was given for breakfast as though the bowl were almost too heavy for him.

The two Arimaspians carried him on toward the northeast all day. The forest of pine and birch grew thicker, closing out the sky, and the land became steadily steeper and

stonier. They were climbing most of the time, and the
ground was rough and uneven. It was difficult for Aristeas
to play sick. When one of the stretcher-bearers stumbled—as they did all the time—he had to remember to
wince as though his head were as sore as it had been the
day before, and this got tiresome. What's more, Skylas,
who was getting tired of carrying the stretcher, kept dropping it to shoot at things with Aristeas's bow. After about
the sixth time he did this, Aristeas started to get bored
with giving agonized groans. Then Skylas always missed
and generally got caught on the arm by the bowstring,
which made him howl with pain, and he seemed to think
it was Aristeas's fault. He'd always jolt the stretcher on
purpose afterward, and that meant more playacted moaning. And Aristeas didn't feel like moaning; he was annoyed
at the way the Arimaspian was treating the bow. It was
the kind of bow people in the east always used then, with
stretchy sinew glued down the back and bits of bone and
horn glued into the front. This made it so stiff that when
it wasn't strung, it actually bent backward, and it was very
powerful for its size, but it also meant that it had to be
looked after properly or it came to pieces. Bows were always kept in cases when they weren't being used because
if the glue was wet for long, it could go soft, and they
were always stored unstrung because otherwise they got
overstretched and went floppy. Skylas, however, never unstrung the bow and never put it away. Aristeas had to keep
reminding himself that it was good that the Arimaspians
broke all the bows they captured, but it still annoyed him.
It was a particularly fine bow, and he was fond of it.

After an extremely slow day's journey the Arimaspians
again made camp. Aristeas was relieved: By this time he
found his own groans totally unconvincing, and he sus-

pected that Hyrgis was starting to do the same.

He'd hoped to be able to question the Arimaspians some more about their queen, Colaxis, and her plans, but instead he found himself being questioned by them. The two were scouts for Colaxis, and it was their business to question intruders on her land. Hyrgis was particularly interested in the parchments in the saddlebags; Skylas wanted to know what enchantment he'd put on the bow. Aristeas swore truthfully that there was no magic in either the book or the bow, but neither of the two believed him.

When the Arimaspians finally left him alone that night, Aristeas badly wanted to escape at once. The trouble was, he still knew very little about Colaxis and her plans, and he had no idea what he'd have to do to stop her. He lay on his back for a while, listening to the Arimaspians snoring and trying to decide what to do. Wasn't what he knew enough? He could just hum a little tune that would make his captors sleep more soundly, then slip off the loose ropes, pick up his saddlebags and his bowcase, and walk off. He'd go back to the Issedones, tell them that there was an Arimaspian plan to enslave them, and then . . .

It wouldn't work. First, the Issedones wouldn't believe him. He wasn't one of their own people, and they thought he was crazy to go into the Arimaspian lands to begin with. Secondly, the Issedones wouldn't want to go to war with the Arimaspians. Despite all their boasts that they weren't afraid of the Arimaspians, it was plain that really they were absolutely terrified of their one-eyed neighbors. As the Arimaspians had grown stronger and more numerous, the Issedones had moved westward, away from them, and this had started a squabbling kind of occasional war with their human neighbors to the west. They wouldn't abandon that, leaving their land unprotected, to fight a desperate battle

against their dreaded one-eyed enemies—not just because
a Greek poet said they should. Thirdly, even if they did
believe Aristeas and did dare to organize an attack, would
it help them? The way they fought was suited to the open
grassland where they lived. They liked to gallop toward an
enemy on their horses, shoot, and gallop off again. In
thickly wooded, mountainous country like this, where they
couldn't use horses and wouldn't get a clear line of shot
for their bows, the Arimaspians would massacre them. In
fact, they'd do better to wait until Colaxis had given her
own followers bows and horses and attacked them. But
they'd probably be defeated then as well, if the Arimaspians really had magic bows as well as their own horrible
strength.

Aristeas stared up at the stars twinkling above him and
cursed. "I'll go back and warn them!" he said. "I'll warn
the Issedones, and then I'll go home. It's not my fault if
they don't believe me. If a whole tribe of horsemen can't
defeat the Arimaspians, how can I? It isn't my business
anyway. Colaxis isn't a threat to my own people. In Proconnesus they don't even believe that Arimaspians exist.
Apollo, if you really want someone to stop Colaxis, pick
one of the Issedones! It's not fair to drag me here from the
other side of the world and expect me to die trying to do
something that's impossible! No, I'll just go home to Proconnesus."

Immediately he felt the old sense that a heartbreaking
disaster was about to occur—the same feeling that had
haunted him day and night in Proconnesus and forced him
to return east. It was worse now, though. Now he knew
what he was afraid of: He could imagine the Arimaspians
killing and eating his Issedonian friends. If he did go home,
he'd never be able to rest. He groaned.

"Very well!" he whispered. "I'll play sick for one more day and see if I can't learn something that will be useful. But I *will* escape after that. I'm not going to allow myself to be carried into the middle of the Arimaspian camp and dropped in front of this Colaxis. Her magic is probably stronger than mine, and even if it isn't, she's got a whole tribe of man-eating giants to protect her. I don't want to be a hero."

The sense of disaster faded. Aristeas rolled onto his side, closed his eyes, and went to sleep angry.

He was still angry next morning. He was getting very tired of dried horsemeat broth and absolutely fed up with Skylas. He stopped groaning when the Arimaspian dropped the stretcher and made nasty remarks instead.

"Don't fly, little bird," he advised when Skylas drew the bow at a blue-tailed bird in the bushes. "Stay right where you are. He's aiming there, and he'll never hit you."

Skylas shot, missed, and caught his arm with the bow-string. He howled, then glared at Aristeas.

"Well done, bowstring!" said Aristeas.

Skylas looked over at Hyrgis. "Can't we cut his tongue out?" he asked.

"No," Hyrgis said firmly. "Colaxis will want him to talk."

"He's casting a spell on me." Skylas rubbed his sore arm.

"No," Hyrgis replied, "you just can't shoot. Nor can I. Another day or two, and the bow will break. It always happens. There's no special magic to it."

"You'd better go fetch the arrow," advised Aristeas. "I think it landed over there, in that thornbush."

Skylas glared some more. "I'm tired of carrying this

human," he told Hyrgis. "He's not ill anymore. He can get up and fetch the arrow, and after that he can walk."

"He's recovering more quickly than I hoped," said Hyrgis, "but he'd probably still faint after a few steps. You're the one who bashed his head in. And if he fainted, he might hit his head again, and this time he might die, and then Colaxis would be angry. No. We carry him. Fetch the arrow yourself if you want it; otherwise leave it. I'd leave it. Human bows are no good for us."

Skylas glowered, picked up his end of the stretcher again, and left the arrow. He deliberately knocked the stretcher against a tree, hard enough that Aristeas didn't have to fake a yelp of pain.

Early in the afternoon they came out of the woodland into an area of dark-leaved bushes and small streams, and when he looked up, Aristeas saw that they'd been climbing the eastern foothills of a great range of mountains. The distant peaks were white with snow and glowed in the light, and the air was cold, clear, and bracing. The Arimaspians seemed nervous in the open and walked quickly. Skylas left the bow—still strung—on top of his pack, and puffed heavily with effort as he climbed, no longer pausing even to bump Aristeas. Soon they began to descend again, going down the northeast flank of the hill, leaving the mountains, and the two seemed more relaxed. Aristeas was sorry to be going back toward the thick woodland, where it was impossible to see any distance ahead. The mountains, bright and sharp and cold, drew him, and he turned his head back to keep his eyes on them as they descended. In the level afternoon light he saw a large bird, surely an eagle, turning on the wind above them. Its wings glinted in the sun as though they were made of gold, and he found himself smiling, a line of poetry forming in his mind. The

eagle drifted toward the mountains, going higher, then disappeared. In a little while, however, it appeared again, this
time with another eagle beside it. They glided closer, de-
scending as though they were deliberately following the
Arimaspians.

Hyrgis glanced over his shoulder and saw the eagles
and, for the first time, dropped the stretcher.

"Griffins!" he shouted, tearing his pack from his
shoulders.

Skylas, too, dropped the stretcher. Aristeas suddenly
remembered the stories he'd heard, how the Arimaspians
were always at war with the gold-hoarding griffins of the
mountains. He tried to sit up, but the straps that fastened
him to the stretcher held him fast.

The two Arimaspians had both shed their packs now
and stood with their long sticks held ready. The griffins
soared directly overhead. Aristeas had a glimpse of the
long, lionlike tails and the bunched foreclaws. They gave a
harsh shriek and turned, flapping their wings to gain
height, then swooped directly upon the Arimaspians.

In the moment that the beasts were turning, Skylas
suddenly dropped his stick and snatched up Aristeas's bow.
As the griffins swept down, he shot, and for some reason—because they were so near, because he wasn't aiming,
because he was lucky—*this* arrow sped true. The second
griffin gave a scream of pain and crumpled sideways upon
one wing, fluttering and falling. The first griffin glanced
back, shrieked in fury, and swept vengefully on. Hyrgis
tensed, leaped aside when it seemed certain that the great
beast's claws would strike him, and brought his stick down
even as he jumped. There was a loud crack! And then the
griffin crashed into the earth next to Aristeas. One golden
wing folded over him, almost shelteringly, and the covert

feathers, smooth and soft as young leaves, brushed his face. The wing was warm, but it did not move.

After a moment the wing was heaved roughly off, and Aristeas saw that the griffin's head was folded under its chest; Hyrgis's blow had broken its neck. But even though it was dead, the Arimaspian struck it again. His yellow teeth were bared in an awful grin as the black club smashed into one of the wings. There was a puff of golden down, and the wing snapped and folded. Skylas yelled with delight and brought his own stick down.

"No!" protested Aristeas. Even dead, the griffin was beautiful, and it tore his heart to see it beaten. But the Arimaspians paid no attention to him. They struck at the animal's body again and again, shouting with a horrible glee, until it was just a mangled pile of broken bones. Then they stopped, looked at each other, and laughed.

"You shot the other one," Hyrgis said suddenly, and they both looked around in the direction where the second griffin had fallen. They both grinned and began running.

"No!" Aristeas shouted again. Without thinking, he tore the ropes off his hands, struggled out of the stretcher, and, kicking one foot free, ran after the Arimaspians with the remaining rope still trailing from one ankle.

He came up behind the two to find them staring into a large dip in the ground where the second griffin lay panting, its injured wing folded beneath it. It gave another harsh shriek and struggled to get to its feet, then fell back onto its side. Hyrgis hefted his stick.

"No," said Skylas, and giggled. "Let me practice on it with the arrows."

Hyrgis laughed. "Yes!" he agreed. "It'll be a long time dying that way."

Skylas picked up the bow again, fitted an arrow, and

aimed. The griffin stared up at him with fierce, brilliant eyes.

Aristeas whistled, and the bowstring snapped. One of its trailing ends lashed back and caught Skylas in the eye, while the arrow spun off sideways and stuck into his sore arm. The Arimaspian howled and jumped up and down, one hand clapped to his face and the other waving the arrow like a flag. Hyrgis spun around. He stared at Aristeas in amazement, for a moment too surprised to move. Aristeas took a deep breath and started to sing.

He sang about mountains, rocks, tall trees with deep roots—anything that is firmly anchored and can't move. The song fixed Hyrgis's feet to the ground. When the Arimaspian tried to rush at his prisoner, he moved as though he were wading in thick mud. Aristeas backed away from him and slowly changed the song. He sang about sleep, the brother of death, easy sleep, that comes winged in night and seals the eyes with rest. Hyrgis first, then Skylas stopped struggling forward, dropped to the ground, and began snoring.

Aristeas stopped singing and shook himself. He felt very tired, too. That wasn't because of the sleep spell, though; that was just from working such a powerful piece of magic. If anyone had asked him if he could put two strong enemies to sleep in the few seconds before they came to kill him, he would certainly have answered that he couldn't.

He went back to the edge of the dip and saw that the griffin was asleep, too. Well, that was just as well. It had been very stupid to rush to the aid of an animal—and one that would probably have killed and eaten him just as happily as it would have killed the Arimaspians. He took the rope off his foot and tied Hyrgis up with it, singing another spell over it to make sure that the prisoner couldn't break free. Then he took the bow away from Skylas, took the broken string off it, and, with great satisfaction, put it safely back in its case.

He walked slowly back to the stretcher and collected his saddlebags. He helped himself to a drink of water from the flask in Hyrgis's pack, then, after sitting still for a couple of minutes to catch his breath, picked up the rest of the rope and returned to the snoring Arimaspians. He tied Skylas up as well. He'd just finished this when he noticed that the griffin had woken up.

He'd seen pictures of griffins hundreds of times. All the people between him and Proconnesus made pictures and carvings of them. Aristeas had seen pouncing griffins carved from stag's horn on knife hilts, griffins swooping on horses worked in gold on sword sheaths, griffins killing lions painted on bowcases. But he'd never spoken to anyone who'd actually *seen* a griffin, and he couldn't resist going a bit nearer.

An eagle's head, wings, and claws on a lion's body: that was how everyone described a griffin. But it wasn't quite true. The griffin was lion-colored and lion-sized, certainly, but not square and tall like a lion. Its body was long and low, more like a leopard's, with powerful hind legs built for jumping, and the tail, shorter and thicker than a lion's, ended not in a tuft of hair but in a spread of feathers. Its forequarters were feathered, too—beautiful golden feathers, with a sheen to them like the sheen on the neck of a rock dove. Aristeas reckoned that the great wings must each be as long as he was tall. There was blood at the base of the left wing and more blood soaking the down on the shoulder, but he couldn't see the arrow; it must be underneath the animal. The curved eagle's beak was agape with pain, but the brilliant dark hawk eyes watched him fiercely, without a trace of fear.

He didn't dare go too near. But if he left the animal lying there, wounded and unable to fly, it would certainly die slowly. It would be kinder to shoot it. Slowly, reluctantly, he took his bow out of its case again and took one of the spare bowstrings from the little oilskin bag beside it. There were only two left; he'd have to make some more. Skylas had lost a number of arrows, too, and he'd had only a dozen. He'd have to retrieve this one after using it. He strung the bow.

He had a sudden peculiar sensation at the front of his head, as though someone had just opened a window in his skull and let in a draft of cold air. There was a kind of flickering picture: himself drawing a bow; an arrow and a sense of impact; blackness; a flash of lightning. It surprised him so much he nearly dropped the bow. There was another flicker: a kind of wing-shaped shadow and a sense of regret. Then himself holding the bow again turning suddenly to an image, seen from the air, of two Arimaspians carrying a stretcher; a face-shaped blur with two eyes; a sense of necessity; a kind of cloud with a sense of power; two face-shaped blurs with one eye each; sleep . . .

The images suddenly seemed to connect inside his mind to words. What had just been said was: "This is the one that was on the stretcher, the two-eyes. He must be a magician, to have put the one-eyes to sleep."

Aristeas stood still a moment, gaping. He looked quickly around; there was no one about but the two snoring Arimaspians.

("I wonder what he's waiting for,") said the flickering. ("He looked as though he meant to shoot me. Isn't he going to?")

Aristeas looked back at the wounded griffin. "Uh," he said, croaking with astonishment, "did you speak?"

("It's making noises at me now,") said the griffin to itself; Aristeas was now sure it was the griffin, talking this peculiar way. ("I wonder why they do that. Come on, two-eyes! Shoot! I don't want to lie here till the one-eyes wake up, and die with them swearing at me.")

Aristeas closed his mouth. He sat down, staring at the griffin. After a moment he closed his eyes and thought a question at it, trying to shoot the query out of his head like an arrow.

The griffin jumped and gave a surprised squawk. ("Is it trying to talk?") it said to itself—the word for *talk* was really more like *flicker*. It picked itself up a little, getting its forelegs underneath itself, and lowered its head, its eyes blinking rapidly. ("Two-eyes, were you talking?")

("Yes,") thought Aristeas, shooting the yes feeling out again.

("Lightning-flash!") said the griffin. It stared at Aristeas, turning its head sideways to fix him with first one eye, then the other. ("Are you—") It hesitated, then produced a complicated idea that he couldn't understand. It seemed to be something about a strong cold wind, with a warm space on the other side of it and a sweet smell.

("?") thought Aristeas.

The griffin repeated the wind and the space behind it, then asked, ("Are you from there?")

"Oh!" Aristeas said, aloud, then, trying to think it in the flickering, ("No.")

("Amazing!") said the griffin. ("Everyone always says that two-eyes can't speak, except possibly the place-beyond-the-wind ones.")

"The Hyperboreans!" Aristeas exclaimed, suddenly understanding. "You mean the Hyperboreans, the people who are said to live beyond the North Wind. Do they really exist then?" Then he had to stop and repeat himself in flicker-talk.

("So it's said,") said the griffin doubtfully. ("But they don't have much to do with anyone else. I've never met one. But they say that the beyond-the-wind ones can speak, and no other humans can. Of course, I've never met a two-eyed human before. One-eyes can hear, but they won't talk. I suppose you can talk because you're a magician. Since you can talk, can you tell me what happened to my mate, Wing-shadow?")

He realized that this must have been the other griffin, and he sat uncomfortably silent for a moment, then sent an image of the Arimaspians hitting with their sticks. The griffin jumped again and gave a long hawklike scream out loud. ("Blackness, lightning-flash!") it shouted in its own language. ("Grief, grief, grief!")

Aristeas covered his ears uselessly. The shout of ("grief!") felt as though it would split his head open. ("Please!") he told the griffin. ("I'm not used to talking like this, and you're hurting me.")

The griffin put its head against its wing and covered its eyes. ("Grief, grief,") it thought, more quietly. ("Wing-shadow! Beautiful sun-glimmer wind-going-up Wing-shadow! . . . Kill me now, two-eyes, send me after her.")

("I'm not going to kill you now,") Aristeas told it—him. ("I was only going to shoot you before because I thought you were an animal.")

The griffin picked his head up again sharply. ("Animal?") he asked in an outraged way.

Aristeas realized he'd produced a kind of four-footed blur rather like a sheep as the word for *animal*. That must be an insult in flicker-talk. He tried again and managed to make it clear that he'd meant an animal that didn't talk.

("But your kind are animals,") said the griffin, with an overtone of bewilderment. The image he used was a warm, furry thing, with a notion of stupidity.

("We are not!") Aristeas told him. ("We can talk perfectly well. But not this way. This is very difficult for me.")

In his grief for his mate, this was too confusing for the griffin to bother with. ("I don't see why the fact that I can speak means you'll leave me to suffer,") he said impatiently.

("I thought you'd kill me if I went near enough to help you,") Aristeas told him. ("Since you're a—a rational being, I can help.")

("My wing's broken,") the griffin replied. ("There's nothing you can do to help—though thank you for offering.")

("But I can help,") Aristeas told him. ("I can heal you. I'm a magician, remember? Let me at least have a look!")

The griffin sent him a doubtful feeling but said, ("Go ahead then. What does it matter?") Aristeas unstrung his bow and put it away again, then ran down the slope to examine the griffin's wound.

The arrow had gone in at the base of the left wing and penetrated through; its point had just pierced the skin by the griffin's shoulder. The wing wasn't broken there but farther up, just above the bend that would be the elbow on a human arm; the griffin must have fallen on it after being shot. There was a lot of blood, and it looked very painful.

("Well?") asked the griffin.

("I've cured worse,") said Aristeas. ("The first thing is to make you comfortable. Then I'll take the arrow out and set the bone. After that")—he couldn't work out how to say "work a healing spell" in flicker-talk, and trying to say anything in the language was very tiring, so he finished—("I'll start to make it better.")

He went back to his saddlebags and fetched his lyre. Several strings were broken, and all were out of tune, so he brought the spare strings, sat down beside the griffin, and began repairing it.

("What's that?") asked the griffin.

("Music maker,") replied Aristeas. He replaced the missing strings and began tuning the instrument. As soon as his hands had touched it, he'd realized that he'd been more furious with Hyrgis for handling it so roughly than he had been with Skylas for the blow on the head. He pulled the strings lovingly, smiling as they sang back to the right pitch.

("It's supposed to make me comfortable?") asked the griffin sarcastically. ("Why do you think I'll like two-eyed music?")

Aristeas didn't answer, merely began to play. The notes rippled out of the lyre like water, and everything around went still. The griffin lay on his good side, watching. After a little while he put his head down on his claws and tucked his good wing up to his chin. His eyelids drooped, and the fierceness went out of his eyes.

("Beautiful,") said the griffin dreamily when Aristeas stopped playing. ("I never would have believed humans could make anything beautiful.")

("Does your wing still hurt?") asked Aristeas.

The griffin picked his head up in surprise and looked at his wing. ("No!") he exclaimed. ("Hardly at all!")

("Good!") said Aristeas. He wrapped the lyre in its oil-skin case and put it back in his saddlebag, then ran back to the stretcher. He had to hurry. It was evening now, and he had to get the arrow out before it became dark. It might be fatal to leave the dart in the griffin's wing overnight.

He fetched Skylas's pack and stopped at the top of the dip to retrieve his knife from Hyrgis's belt. The Arimaspians were still sleeping peacefully. Aristeas took his copper cooking pot from the pack, filled it with water from the flask, and took it down into the dip. He collected some kindling and lit a fire with flints, then set the water on to heat. Quickly he cut the tail feathers off the arrow and drew it out of the wing by the point. In spite of the spell, the griffin tensed when he pulled it and gave a squawk of pain, but then it was over. The water was boiling, and Aristeas threw some salt in it to purify it further. He cut a piece from Skylas's spare deerskin tunic and used it to clean the wound and used the rest of the tunic as a bandage, tying it down firmly to stop any more bleeding. Then he turned his attention to the broken bone. He was working by firelight now, but this job was one that was better done by touch anyway. He set the bone straight and splinted it with branches cut from one of the dark-leaved shrubs, and that was that. Now he should work a healing spell. But he realized he'd never be able to. He was far too tired.

The griffin ran his beak along the splint and straightened some of his feathers. ("How wonderful!") he said. ("I've never heard of this sort of magic. Will these sticks melt into my wing if I fly?")

("Magic?") said Aristeas. ("I haven't done any yet—except the spell to stop it hurting. Your bone will set straight now, that's all. But I can't do any more just now. I must rest.")

He knew, though, that he couldn't rest yet; there were a few more things still to do. Wearily he washed his hands

in the pot of water, which had grown lukewarm again. He
went back up and checked on the Arimaspians. They were
still snoring happily. After a minute he pulled a hide blanket out of the pack and put it over Skylas. The night was
cold, up here on the mountainside, and he didn't want
them to freeze. He had some questions he wanted to ask
them. He trekked back to the stretcher to fetch Hyrgis's
pack and hide blanket as well. The mangled remains of the
dead griffin were still lying beside the stretcher, looking
even more broken and forlorn by the gray light of the half-
moon. He stood still for a minute, looking at them. There
lay beautiful sun-glimmer, wind-going-up Wing-shadow.

He picked up the stretcher, set it over the twisted body,
and weighted the edges with stones. That would keep her
safe for now, and in the morning the living griffin could
tell him how the body should be buried.

He dragged the heavy pack back to the dip in the hillside and threw a blanket over Hyrgis. He thought about
boiling up some more dried horsemeat, but he was much
too tired. He collected his own blanket and looked around
for a good place to sleep. The mountains stood tall behind
him, their snow-covered peaks gleaming in the moonlight,
and a cold wind slipped from them along the ground. Aristeas shivered, suddenly feeling horribly alone. There
wasn't another human being within a hundred miles of
him now—unless you counted as human the two Arimaspians, lumpish in their blankets on the edge of the dip. He
pulled his blanket over his shoulders and walked down the
slope to the griffin.

("Do you mind if I sleep down here near you?") he
asked.

The griffin had been sitting with his head against his
wing, grieving, but he picked himself up. ("No, not at

all,") he said. After a moment he added, ("Do you have a name, two-eyes?")

"Aristeas," he said aloud.

The griffin cocked his head and fixed one eye on him. Aristeas realized that his name was just a meaningless noise as far as the griffin was concerned.

("My name is Ar-is-te-as,") he repeated. He had to think out the sounds one by one.

("Sounds? Your kind uses sounds for names?") asked the griffin.

("That's the way we talk.")

("How strange! Talking with sounds! I never thought of that.") He paused, then added, almost shyly, ("My name is Firegold.") The name was really an image, a combination of fire and metal. ("I can't say that Arrri-business. Doesn't your name mean anything?")

"Umm." Aristeas hesitated in embarrassment, then admitted, ("Well, yes. It means . . . well, 'best'—'excellent,' that is, or 'bravest.'")

Firegold seemed impressed. ("Excellent! That's a very distinguished name. Did your people give you that title?")

("No—just my father. He was")—Aristeas stopped and helplessly finished aloud—"aristocratic."

("What?")

Aristeas thought of the complicated politics of his own Greek city and its endless squabbles over systems of government. He tried to imagine how to say *democracy* in flicker-talk. (Taking-directions-from-crowds? Paying-attention-to-most-people?) He groaned. ("I can't explain,") he said firmly, ("and I want to go to sleep.") He lay down and rolled himself in the blanket.

("Excellent,") said Firegold as he tried to find a comfortable place to lie, ("why did you save my life?")

("?") said Aristeas irritably.

("You stopped whatever you were doing on that stretcher and attacked the two one-eyes when they were going to kill me. And now you're healing me from a deadly wound. Why?")

Aristeas remembered the moment when he'd stood facing the two furious Arimaspians. This time he was horrified at himself for flinging himself after them that way, without so much as a dagger to defend himself! He saw Hyrgis turning, his yellow teeth bared as his jaw dropped in astonishment. By Apollo! he thought, feeling cold all over. I could have been killed! I was closer to death than when Skylas hit me!

He shivered, opening his eyes and looking out at the night to block out the picture of the Arimaspians' glaring eyes and dripping teeth. ("I don't know why I did it,") he told Firegold. ("They're enemies to my kind and . . . I didn't want them to kill you. I hated it when they killed your mate.")

("Then why didn't you kill them?")

("I couldn't. I have to follow rules when I work magic.")

("Rules?")

("I'll explain tomorrow. For now I must sleep. Good night.")

("Excellent, first I must thank you for my life. I will repay the debt honorably.")

("Good! Let me sleep! Good night!")

He fell asleep before Firegold could say anything else. Halfway through the night he woke shivering and turned over into something warm. When he woke again at dawn, he found that he was pressed against the griffin's side, tucked securely under the golden wing.

What Do You
Intend to Do?

3

It was the noise that woke Aristeas up. Horrible howls and
bellows of rage resounded from the mountains; the two
Arimaspians had finally awoken.

Firegold jumped to his feet, then gave a squawk of pain
as the movement hurt his wound. Aristeas stumbled
quickly up the slope.

He'd tied Hyrgis and Skylas like goats in a market, with
their hands and feet together, because he'd been a bit short
of rope. The two now lay on their sides, kicking their legs
and twisting their arms as they struggled to free themselves. It was Skylas who was doing most of the yelling;
Hyrgis was using all his strength on the rope.

"Stop that at once!" ordered Aristeas.

The two paused and looked toward him. Hyrgis's eye
was burning with rage like a red-hot coal, but Skylas's was
bleared and swollen, and he didn't seem to be able to see
properly, because he looked over to one side of Aristeas
rather than directly at him. The snapped bowstring must
have done more damage than Aristeas had realized.

"You liar!" howled Skylas, starting to struggle again.
"You miserable cheat! You swore that bow wasn't magic!"

"It isn't," Aristeas told him calmly. Skylas only swore more loudly.

"Ignore him," panted Hyrgis, beginning to strain at the rope again. "We can break these. I don't know why they haven't broken already."

"They haven't broken because I've enchanted them," Aristeas informed him helpfully.

Hyrgis stopped struggling and glared at Aristeas again. "You're a magician," he said accusingly.

"By Apollo!" replied Aristeas in pretended astonishment. "However did you work that out? Skylas, stop shouting, or I'll enchant away your voice."

Skylas stopped shouting with a whimper. "I wish I had killed you!" he said with deep feeling.

"You did your best," said Aristeas, "but I'll overlook that. I could leave both of you here to starve, but I won't. If you do as I say, I may even let you go free."

Hyrgis gave him a look so full of hatred that Aristeas took a step backward. "Spy!" hissed the Arimaspian. "That's why you came to our country, wasn't it? To spy out the secrets of Colaxis!" Then his savage expression changed. "Where are you really from?" he demanded, suddenly unsure of himself. "Are you from—there?"

"Where?" asked Aristeas, puzzled.

"North Wind." Hyrgis said it in a whisper. "The place beyond it."

That was immensely interesting. Not that Hyrgis, too, should suspect Aristeas of being a Hyperborean—the race was famous for magic, so it was a natural assumption. No, what was interesting was that the Arimaspian was so obviously afraid of the Hyperboreans. Maybe the place to look for help against Colaxis was beyond the North Wind. If he could get there. "No," he answered Hyrgis, though reluctantly. "I told you, I'm a Greek."

("Excellent,") came a call in flicker-talk, and Aristeas glanced around and saw that Firegold had struggled up to the top of the dip. The griffin was standing on three legs, the foreclaw on his bad side pulled up to his chest. His tail was twitching, and the feathers on the top of his head were standing up. The Arimaspians winced when he spoke, and both looked toward him with absolute loathing.

("Excellent,") Firegold said again, ("are you going to kill them now?")

("No,") said Aristeas.

Skylas gave a yelp. "Make it stop!" he shouted. "It hurts my eye! Even you can't like the monster, human! Vicious creatures, no good even for eating! Kill the brute, kill it!"

("Excellent, if you don't want to kill them yourself, may I ask—may I ask you to give them to me?")

"Don't you understand what he's saying?" Aristeas asked Skylas.

"They don't say anything," whined Skylas. "They just put hot lights in my poor eye, and it hurts."

("Excellent, they killed my mate,") said Firegold urgently. ("Let me avenge her! Untie them, and I will strike them both to the ground!")

("No!") Aristeas said firmly. ("I won't untie them, or they'd strike *us* to the ground. And we can't kill them.")

Hyrgis gave a sudden jump. "That wasn't the griffin!" he exclaimed. "That was you, human. You can talk to the beast; you *are* from there!"

The griffin lashed his tail. He turned his head sideways, as he seemed to do whenever he wanted to stare hard at something. ("Last night I thought you were their enemy,") he said to Aristeas angrily.

Aristeas looked back at Firegold irritably. Last night I

thought you were my friend, he thought—but to himself.
This morning he wasn't so sure. After all, why should he
trust a griffin?

"Make it stop!" wailed Skylas again.

"What do *those* people want with us?" asked Hyrgis
nervously.

("What are they saying to you, in that sound-language?") demanded Firegold.

"Oh, be quiet!" snapped Aristeas. "I can't talk two lan-
guages to three of you at once." He took a deep breath.
("Firegold, I am their enemy. But I cannot kill them. Even
if there weren't other reasons, I can't kill them because I
need to question them.")

("About what?") Firegold clenched the earth with his
talons, the feathers now standing up all the way down his
neck. ("What are you plotting with them, in your sound-
language?")

("They have a ruler who is a witch. She plans to use
her powers against their enemies; she's making magic bows
that they can use and—")

Firegold's wings spread with a whoosh, and his feathers
all stood on end. ("Bows?") he shouted, so forcefully that
Aristeas winced, too. ("The one-eyes have their own bows?
Blackness! Many dead! Pain!")

Skylas gave another howl, and Aristeas put his hands
over his eyes, which was no more use than putting them
over his ears. ("Stop!") he told Firegold. ("You're hurting
me again.")

Firegold took no notice. He reared up on his hind legs,
shaking his pinions. The wind of them shook the bushes,
and the open wings made him seem enormous, like a ship
in full sail. ("So that is how they could strike me yesterday!") he exclaimed. ("They have bows of their own. I

thought they just had a stolen one. And that is why Wing-shadow died! She was angry because they'd wounded me, she forgot to be careful, she flew at them. She died, and I was wounded, because the one-eyes have bows!")

("*These* one-eyes did just have a stolen bow yester-day—my bow. I don't know anything about the other bows, except that one of these two was boasting that their queen had made some. If you don't settle down, I'll have to reset that wing bone!")

Firegold folded his wings. Then, stiffly, he bowed his head and touched it to Aristeas's foot. ("Forgive me, Excellent! It was my heart's grief that made me accuse you of plotting with the one-eyes. They must indeed live and tell you everything. This is the worst news I have ever heard. With bows the one-eyes could wipe my kind out.")

And Aristeas realized that that was true. All the stories he'd heard said that the Arimaspians and the griffins were constantly at war, and he had seen a skirmish in that war for himself the day before. But it must, until now, have been a stalemate: In wooded country the Arimaspians had the advantage, but on the bare mountain slopes the griffins could usually destroy their enemies easily. Arimaspians with bows would change that. Aristeas felt suddenly much happier. Firegold really was his ally against Colaxis.

("Can I leave you here on guard then?") he asked Firegold. ("I need to fetch us some water, and it would be good if I could shoot something for breakfast. The only thing these two have to eat is dried horsemeat.")

("Disgusting!") said Firegold. ("But I thought you were going to heal my wing.")

("After breakfast. Working magic is very tiring, and I want something to eat first.")

Firegold settled himself on the top of the dip, putting

his beak to his claws and wrapping his tail under his chin like a cat. ("I will keep them safe,") he promised solemnly.

("Good!") Aristeas fetched his copper cooking pot and the water flasks, then picked up his bowcase. "Hyrgis and Skylas," he called, and the two Arimaspians glowered at him. "This is Firegold," he told them. "I'm leaving him in charge of you. You killed his mate yesterday, and he'd love to get revenge, so don't do anything to annoy him. I'll be back soon."

He found a stream of clean mountain water not far away and filled the pot and the water flasks. He left them on a flat rock by the water and crept a bit farther, looking for game. He hadn't gone two hundred paces up the stream when he surprised a flock of wild sheep drinking at a pool. They bounded off, but not before he put an arrow into one of them. He staggered back to the others with the sheep over his shoulders, the pot in one hand, and the water flasks hanging from the other, feeling very pleased with himself.

("Well hunted!") exclaimed Firegold, looking at the sheep with his beak agape hungrily. ("I love mutton. May I share your kill?")

("Of course,") Aristeas said graciously. "Umm . . . (do your people cook your food? Or not?")

("Cook?") The griffin repeated the image of roasting meat in horror. ("You put good meat in a fire? Lightning-flash!")

("Not,") Aristeas observed. ("Well, take what you want first. I'm going to cook mine.")

In a few minutes he had some mutton steaks, rolled around thyme and juniper berries, roasting over a fire in the bottom of the dip. Firegold sat beside him, tearing a haunch of mutton into strips and swallowing them and occasionally shaking his head over the awful waste of good meat.

The two Arimaspians lay at the top of the slope, securely tied up. Skylas began to mutter mournfully to himself that he was starving, that the human was sitting there stuffing himself, and his own stomach was so empty it was full of cobwebs, that he was going to lie there and die, with the smell of delicious fresh meat all around him. Hyrgis told him to be quiet.

"You can have some later," Aristeas called up to them, taking a steak off the fire and juggling it from hand to hand while it cooled, "as soon as I feel up to dealing with you."

("What?") asked Firegold. He was still unhappy when Aristeas spoke to the Arimaspians in "sound-language." From his point of view, one-eyes and two-eyes were very much alike, and conversations between them made him nervous.

("I said I'd feed them later,") Aristeas told him. He took a big bite of mutton. It was delicious.

("Feed them? Why? They don't deserve food, certainly not good food like this.")

Aristeas sighed. ("I know. But I got the better of them by magic, and I mean to go on using magic to manage them, so I have to treat them well. It's one of the rules.")

("What rules? Excellent, I owe you a debt for my life, and if there really is a wicked plot by a one-eye ruler to arm her people with bows, all my kind will be grateful to you for exposing it, but you're going to have to explain things if I'm to trust you. When Wing-shadow and I first saw you, we thought you were the one-eyes' prisoner, but after they attacked us, you freed yourself and had them helpless in minutes. Why couldn't you do that *before* they shot me? Then Wing-shadow would still be alive. You treat me like a friend, but you also refuse to hurt the one-eyes. And you say you're not from beyond the wind, but you're a powerful magician, and you speak our language. Who are you? Why have you come here? What do you intend to do now?")

Aristeas chewed his meat slowly, then had a drink of water from the flask. ("I'll try to explain,") he said at last, ("but it isn't easy. I don't really understand what's been happening myself. Do your people have . . . divinities?")

("Divinities?") repeated Firegold, puzzled by the word, which Aristeas had had to invent. Then: ("Oh! You mean, Do we worship the gods? Of course we do. Don't your kind?")

("Yes,") Aristeas said, relieved. ("The one-eyes don't. Well, nine years ago I was living at home in my own city of Proconnesus, a Greek city on an island in the Sea of Marmara.") He was aware the names wouldn't mean anything to Firegold, but then the image "city" probably wouldn't either; there were no cities for thousands of miles. He was going to have to invent image-words for things as he went along, and Firegold was just going to have to understand as much as he could. ("I was young and just starting to compose poetry. I badly wanted to be a famous poet, and I used to pray to the god we call Apollo, who's god of poetry, among other things, and beg him to give me a gift. I promised him that I would serve him as long as I lived, and do whatever he wanted me to, if he'd give me a real gift. Well, one day in early spring, nine years ago, around about noon, I went into a shop to pick up some woolen cloth for my mother. I'd been feeling very odd all morning, I remember, as though there were a thunderstorm about to burst inside my head. I was standing there, waiting for the shopkeeper to fetch the cloth, when suddenly it was as though a lightning flash struck me inside.") He stopped, then went on: ("That was how it was for me, that is. They told me afterward that I'd dropped dead.")

("Dead?") asked Firegold in bewilderment.

("Yes. The shopkeeper thought I'd fainted, at first, and threw cold water on me and so on, but then he checked to see if I was breathing, and as far as he could tell, I wasn't. So he locked up his shop and ran to find my family. Meanwhile, I'd found myself outside the city gates—")

("Meanwhile? You mean, while you were dead?")

("Yes. I know it sounds ridiculous, but I must have been there at the same time as I was lying on the shop floor apparently dead. I met one of my father's friends on the road outside the gates, and he started talking to me, asking me about my family and how everyone was getting on. It took me a bit of time to get away from him. When I did, he went on into the city and met my father in the marketplace about the same time as the shopkeeper came running up with the news that I'd just dropped dead, and he and the shopkeeper had a furious argument, with the shopkeeper saying I was dead and my father's friend saying I wasn't. Eventually everyone went back to the shop, but when the shopkeeper unlocked the door, the room was empty. They told me all this when I went back two years ago. Anyhow, I'd started running east. My mind was all muddled from the lightning, but I felt as though there'd just been a dreadful accident, and I must help. I ran until everything around me went into a mist, and I fell over.

("When I woke up, I felt as if I'd been dragged behind a chariot, and there was a tribe of Scythian nomads standing all around me staring. They said I'd fallen from a cloud, and at first they thought I was a god. When I spoke to them in Greek, though, they decided that I'd just been touched by a god and wasn't one myself; they're quite certain that the gods only speak Scythian. But they were very kind to me, even though they don't usually like foreigners. When I left, they gave me a horse, a bow, and some supplies. I had nothing with me except my lyre, which I'd been carrying when I went into the wool shop. They told me that I was at the other end of the Euxine Sea, hundreds of miles from Proconnesus, and I set out from there for the northeast. I still had the feeling that something terrible had happened or was happening, and that I had to help.

("I traveled for years. Every time I tried to turn aside, I was so tormented with anxiety about this unknown disaster that I couldn't rest and had to go on. After five years of it I reached the lands of the Issedones, just to the southwest of here, but there I decided to stop. From what the Issedones told me, I'd reached the end of the earth, and there were no human tribes beyond, only one-eyes and griffins, and maybe the place beyond the wind, if that is on the earth and not somewhere past the edge of it. So I pushed the feeling of disaster aside and started home.

("After two years I got back to Proconnesus, and after one month I couldn't stand the anxiety and had to leave again. This time I gave up fighting the god, and went straight on northeast into the one-eyes' country. Hyrgis and Skylas met up with me a few days ago. They knocked me on the head, almost killing me, and it took me a couple of days to heal myself and recover the use of my powers, which is why I didn't escape earlier. They were bringing me to their queen so she could question me and then eat me; it seems they all love the taste of human flesh. As for why I didn't try to help when you first attacked them—I'm sorry. I didn't realize that griffins were anything more than animals, and it happened so fast. Anyway, while I was recovering, I learned what I've just told you, that the queen of the one-eyes is a powerful witch who's planning ruin for her neighbors. I'm sure that that is the disaster the god wants me to try to prevent, though how I'm supposed to do it, I have no idea. But it seems that she became queen at just the time—at the time I was first struck down with this wretched magic that's blighted my life ever since.")

("You say that as though you hate it,") said Firegold.

("I do! Oh, I admit, when I first realized that the god had given me not just poetry but magic powers I was delighted. I felt it made me better than ordinary people. And it was fun traveling at first—seeing all the different tribes, singing for their rulers, and getting gifts of gold and horses. But after a year or two I wanted to go home.

("I miss Proconnesus. I miss my family and my friends. Do you know, my mother died while I was away the first time? My own mother! It was five years after I left the city, and I wasn't even there to say good-bye! And when I was back two years ago, my father hadn't been well. It helped him just to see me. He was so pleased and so full of plans for what we would do, now he had his son and heir back. And a month later I had to go again. The gods know how he took it. I'm sick of living among barbarians, sleeping in a wagon or a felt tent or in a blanket on the cold ground. I'd give all the gold in the world for a hot bath, a loaf of good wheat bread, and a chance to sleep in a real bed in a real bedroom with floors! If I could renounce magic forever and go home as a perfectly ordinary citizen of Proconnesus, I'd do it in an instant. But I can't.")

("Is that one of the rules you were talking about?")

("Yes,") Aristeas said gloomily. ("The trouble with this magic is, I can't do anything with it that offends the god who gave it to me. And he's the god of healing, music, and light; he doesn't like death. He may destroy things himself, but whatever I use his power on is under his protection afterward, and I'm not allowed to harm it. For example, I'm not allowed to kill anyone by magic. If I try, it just won't work. What's more, I can't even kill someone by normal means after casting a spell on them, no matter what they want to do to me. Once I was set on by bandits. There were a dozen of them. I slowed them down with a spell, the way I fixed Hyrgis and Skylas to the ground yesterday, and while they were trying to shake their feet loose, I tried to shoot them. The moment I drew my bow, I fell off my horse in a dead faint, and when I woke up next day, I was so sick I could barely move.")

("What happened to the . . . bandits?") asked Firegold, hesitating before the word as though he weren't quite sure what it meant.

("They stole practically everything I owned,") Aristeas said bitterly. ("I'd been given many presents by a king who'd liked my singing, and they took the lot. Five horses, a beautiful big tent, a golden bowl, a sword with a ruby hilt, a jeweled dagger—everything. They left only my lyre and my bow and a few other things they had no use for. The only reason they didn't take my life as well was that they thought I was dead already.")

("Maybe you were.")

("Are you making fun of me?") Aristeas asked suspiciously. ("It's not funny at all! I've done the dying business a couple of times since the first time, and I hate it. But I didn't do it then.")

Firegold ruffled his feathers. ("That's an extraordinary story,") he said. ("If I hadn't seen your magic for myself, I wouldn't believe you.")

("Thank you very much! A griffin doesn't believe me! Back in Proconnesus they don't believe in you!")

("I said if I hadn't seen the magic!") Firegold said hastily. ("I'm not calling you a liar, Excellent.")

("It's very hard for me to tell a lie,") Aristeas replied irritably. ("The god doesn't like it. He never tells lies, though he's often very misleading. If I tell a lie, I feel thoroughly sick afterward. It's a terrible nuisance, especially for a Greek poet. Mine isn't the most truthful trade or nation to belong to.") He'd finished his mutton, and he licked the juice off his hands and got up to put the cooking pot full of water on the embers of the fire.

("So,") said Firegold, after a minute or so of silence, ("what *do* you intend to do now?")

("I have no idea!") replied Aristeas, still irritated. ("Apollo expects me to do something about this Queen Colaxis, so I suppose I have to see if there's anything I can do. I'm not in any hurry to meet her, though. I was thinking maybe I could see if these beyond-the-wind people would help. Do you know how to find them?")

("Find them?") said Firegold. ("I've never heard of anyone who's ever found them. The stories say they've passed through our lands and other lands on their way about the world, but all those stories are from long ago. I don't think anyone alive has ever seen one of the beyond-the-wind people. And even in a story I've never heard of anyone visiting their country and coming back. I suppose they live to the north, but how anyone would reach them, I don't know.")

("O Apollo! I don't know what to do then. Let me take things one step at a time! Today I have to heal your wing and work out how to handle the one-eyes. And I thought you might want to, umm, deal with your mate's body according to your own customs. That's enough to keep us busy for now.")

At the mention of his mate Firegold looked miserable. ("Poor Wing-shadow!") he said. ("Is—is her body safe?")

("Yes, I put it under the stretcher. Let's get to work on your wing, and then you can help me do . . . whatever needs to be done.") Aristeas picked up his lyre and checked that it was still in tune.

"Oi, human!" shouted Skylas. "I thought you said you were going to feed us!"

"I said, when I was feeling up to dealing with you," returned Aristeas. "And I'll feel much better about that with Firegold here restored to full health. If you keep quiet and listen, I'll heal your eye as well."

"I hate music!" complained Skylas. But he was quiet.

Aristeas played the healing music on his lyre. He knew at once that the magic was particularly powerful for some reason; he could feel its strength going out like a stream of warmth from a fire, settling over Firegold in a shower of invisible sparks. The griffin sat very still, his eyes deep and dreamy. He remained still, staring into nothing, even after the music was finished. Aristeas got up and checked the splinted wing. The bone had knitted quite smooth, whole, and straight under the golden feathers. He was impressed by it; usually he had to play several times to cure someone. He took off the splint, then knelt and began unfastening the bandage, and Firegold finally shook himself, ruffled his feathers, then looked at his own side as the cut and bloodstained tunic came off. The raw wound was now reduced to two small scars, one below the wing, one on the shoulder.

Firegold stared at it in awe. ("You must be the most powerful magician since Gold-arrow of the beyond-the-wind people!") he said.

("Who?") said Aristeas. But he felt smug. He went to check on the Arimaspians.

They, too, were in a kind of daze, but when he stopped beside them, they came out of it with a jump. Skylas's eye was better and now glared as angrily as Hyrgis's.

"Horrible!" wailed Skylas. "That was horrible! I feel all weak!"

"Music!" snarled Hyrgis. "You work your magic with music." He shuddered with disgust.

Aristeas looked at him indignantly, but before he'd thought of anything to say, Firegold came up behind him in one great leap with spread wings. ("Do we question them now?") he asked eagerly.

("I think we'd better feed them first,") said Aristeas. ("I'll cut up that tunic we were using as a bandage and tie their feet; that will leave them free to hold their food with their hands. You'll have to stand over them while I untie and retie their hands, though.")

Firegold stood over the Arimaspians eagerly. He stood over them so close he was resting a claw on their shoulders and the tip of his curved beak on Hyrgis's throat. Neither of them made any trouble. Aristeas tied their feet with strips cut from the tunic and pulled a loop of rope from their hands around their necks, so that they couldn't reach down to untie the knots that held their feet. Then he gave the two some mutton.

("And now,") he told Firegold, ("I'm going to wash. I've been wearing this same tunic for five days now, and it's stiff enough to stand up by itself.")

He walked down to the pot of water, which was now nicely hot, and took off his cloak, tunic, and trousers.

Firegold gave a caw of astonishment. ("You can take your skin off!") he cried.

Aristeas gave him a withering look. ("Clothes, Firegold, clothes! Don't you even know about those?") There was something on his head, and he pulled it off, too, and found that it was the old deerskin bandage. There was a lot of dried blood on it. He tossed it aside distastefully and began splashing water over his head. Firegold watched, turning his head from one side to the other, utterly fascinated.

("Aren't you going to take off the black fur headpiece as well?") he asked.

("That's my hair.") He shook himself, dried himself with the dirty tunic, and tossed it in the cooking pot to soak in the warm water.

Firegold made a sort of flicker that didn't seem to mean anything, a bright, stammering sort of flicker. Aristeas looked at him sharply. ("What was that?") he demanded.

("Nothing,") said Firegold.

("Were you laughing at me?")

("It's because you're cooking your skin. It seems funny.")

Aristeas took the spare tunic out of his saddlebags, put it on, and belted it with an injured air.

("Well, it does!") protested Firegold. ("The whole situation seems funny. Here you are, a great magician sent by a god to deliver my people, and you pause from working magic to cook your skin . . . what's the matter?")

Aristeas was staring at him with his mouth gaping like a fish. ("What you said,") he told the griffin. ("The god sent me to deliver your race. And he did. The Issedones as well, but your people, too . . . If they believe me about the bows, would they be willing to fight the one-eyes?")

("Of course,") said Firegold. ("There's nothing else we can do. I was intending to fly back to them and tell them everything as soon as I could. But I—I was hoping you might come, too. If this witch is really very powerful . . . would you help us?")

("Yes! Of course! I'll handle the witch if your people handle the rest of the man-eaters. Wonderful, by Apollo, absolutely wonderful!")

("What?")

("For nine years this disaster has haunted me, and now, finally, I can see a way to be rid of it forever. Wonderful!") He turned toward the west and gave a whoop of joy. "Proconnesus!" he shouted. "I'll be coming home!"

The Journey to the Boundary

4

The rest of the day was less satisfying. Wing-shadow's funeral was harder to arrange than Aristeas had expected.

("We must take her body home,") said Firegold very firmly, ("and leave it for Lightning-flash on Sky-fire Mountain.")

("For lightning flash?") asked Aristeas, confused.

("Yes—the god. You were talking about him, too, weren't you?")

("I don't think so,") Aristeas said doubtfully.

("But you said")—Firegold produced an image of music and light in a sense of power—("sent you.") Aristeas realized he had been using the same image himself, as well as the god's name. ("That has to be Lightning-flash,") the griffin finished confidently. ("We call him that, too, sometimes.")

("I was talking about Apollo,") Aristeas replied. ("We believe that the lightning belongs to another god. But I suppose Apollo might use lightning here, even if he doesn't in Greece. Where is this mountain?")

("In the Shoulder of the World—the heart of our country, that is, the high mountains. Lightning-flash loves it and makes the lightning dance there whenever the storms come. We always bring the bodies of our dead there.")

("But—but how far away is it?")

("Four, maybe five days' flying.")

("Can you carry her that far?")

Firegold fluffed up his neck feathers anxiously. No bird can fly carrying more than its own weight, and, as Aristeas had suspected, it was obviously the same with griffins. ("I know!") Firegold exclaimed after a moment's thought. ("You can cast a spell on her to make her light!")

("No, I can't!") said Aristeas. ("Enchantment of the dead is necromancy, a very black kind of magic, and Apollo strictly forbids it. I'd probably fall down in fits if I even thought about it hard.")

Firegold lowered the feathers on his head. After a moment he raised them again. ("If you could summon the lightning here, then we wouldn't need to bring her to Sky-fire Mountain. We could move her body to the top of this hill, and then—")

("I'm sorry, but I don't know any spells to control the weather either. Does the body need to be struck by lightning? Wouldn't . . . well, wouldn't it do just to burn it?")

("No!") said Firegold in distress. ("We all want our bodies taken by Lightning-flash, and our spirits set free on the Sky-fire. It's what Wing-shadow wanted.")

("But what if someone dies when there isn't any lightning storm?") asked Aristeas.

("We wait until there is,") said Firegold. ("We leave the bodies in the snow of the high peaks while we're waiting. They can rest safely there for years.")

He flopped down on his belly and put his head against his wing. ("Oh, blackness!") he said miserably. ("Lovely Wing-shadow dead, and not even the white wings of the lightning to speed her on her way heavenward. Dark earth, foul smoke, red burning!")

Aristeas felt ashamed of himself. He sat down beside the griffin. ("Aren't there any of your own kind closer than the Shoulder of the World?") he asked. ("Couldn't you ask for help?")

Firegold rubbed his wing with his beak. ("There's a hunting party six or seven hours' flight east of here. But they wouldn't be allowed to come this far west. Wing-shadow and I were scouts; we'd been sent to see whether the area was safe to hunt or whether it was being used by the one-eyes. The hunting party are all youngsters. They have to have the First Ones' permission to come as far as this. And to get that, they'd have to go to the Shoulder of the World and come back. We can't keep the body that long.")

("But we could take the body to them on the stretcher. And maybe you could fetch them a couple of hours toward us.")

Firegold picked up his head, and his crest feathers rose again. ("And then they could help carry Wing-shadow the rest of the way! Could you take the stretcher by yourself?")

("Probably not,") admitted Aristeas. ("But we could make the one-eyes help.")

Firegold agreed to this eagerly. They went together to arrange the corpse on the stretcher. Seeing his mate's mangled body was extremely distressing for Firegold, and Aristeas eventually left him to grieve. He came back to the dip and looked hard at the two Arimaspians, who were now sitting up and whispering together. The next job was to question them.

He picked up his lyre and sat down near the two.

"What are you doing now?" demanded Hyrgis suspiciously.

Aristeas began to play without answering, pulling the strings gently so they gave off little runs of notes, like a blackbird.

"It's more magic, isn't is?" said Hyrgis. "I know! You want to cast a spell on us so that we'll tell you more about Colaxis! Skylas, shout! Shout loud! Drown . . . him . . . out . . ." Hyrgis trailed off dazedly for a moment, then shook himself and started shouting.

Skylas joined him for a minute or two, then trailed off, gaping stupidly. Hyrgis shouted on by himself for a little while but finally fell silent, mouth open and eye dim.

Firegold swept up, flying low with rapid wingbeats. ("I heard the one-eyes shouting,") he said anxiously, ("and . . . oh! What have you done to them?")

("We can question them now,") said Aristeas.

Hyrgis and Skylas answered Aristeas's questions in flat, mumbling voices as though they were talking in their sleep. What they had to say was frightening.

Colaxis was planning an attack on the griffins in about a month's time and an assault on the Issedones at the end of the summer. Though she'd been queen of the Arimaspians for nine years, for a long time most of her attention had been taken up by her enemies within the tribe. However, she'd destroyed the last of these—her elder brother—four years before and had been plotting against the tribe's enemies since.

She'd seen at once that the key to defeating both the griffins and the Issedones was the use of bows, but at first she hadn't been able to make any that her followers could use. Last year, though, she'd found a way of making magic bows that did not break and always hit their mark, no matter how clumsy the archer who used them. Colaxis had managed to equip her own bodyguard of a hundred warriors with the magic bows, and she was making more for picked fighters among the rest of the tribe. Hyrgis had hoped to get one, as he was one of her favorite scouts and had been doing some special spying for her on the expedition with Skylas that his partner didn't know about. He said that Colaxis wanted to have another two hundred magic bows ready by the time she attacked the griffins.

The only hopeful knowledge was that there weren't actually as many Arimaspians as Aristeas had feared. The warriors, who were both men and women, numbered about two thousand. The tribe lived in much the same way as the Issedones or most of the other people Aristeas had visited. They used tents instead of houses and kept herds of horses, sheep, and goats, which they drove about wherever the grazing was good. The Arimaspians' two-eyed ancestors had ridden the horses, but all animals were terrified of the one-eyes, and the horses were now kept only for their meat. Colaxis, though, had been trying to cast spells on some of the animals to tame them and hoped to have horses ready to take Arimaspian riders by the end of the summer. She'd chosen a site for the main Arimaspian camp with horse taming in mind; it was beside a large lake on the edge of the grasslands, some four days' journey to the north.

Aristeas translated all this information for Firegold, then sat looking thoughtfully at the two spellbound Arimaspians. "What were you whispering about just now?" he asked them.

"We were discussing how to kill the human," replied Skylas in the flat mumble.

"And how were you going to do that?"

"Hyrgis says he can understand a little of the griffin-talk. He says we must wait until we know the griffin is away somewhere, and then he'll ask the human for a drink of water. The human will have to step between us, and when he bends over to give Hyrgis the water, I have to kick him so he falls on top of Hyrgis. Then Hyrgis will be able to strangle him. Hyrgis says the human won't be able to work magic while he's being strangled; he needs his voice or the music thing for that."

Aristeas let out his breath in a whistle, and he translated for Firegold.

"Hyrgis," he went on, "how much of the flicker-talk do you understand?"

"Only a little," mumbled Hyrgis. "At first it was all hot lights and no sense. But now I can see it's words. They were speaking about the other griffin, the dead one, wanting to take it somewhere. They don't know I understand anything. I'll catch them by surprise soon."

Aristeas began playing the lyre again.

("What's that for?") asked Firegold eagerly. ("Will it turn them into your slaves?")

("No!") Aristeas said impatiently. ("This is just to calm my nerves. Spells to steal away an enemy's will and enslave him are black magic, and I keep telling you, I can't do that. There's no need to worry; when I break this spell, they won't remember anything they've said, and if they think their scheme has a chance of working, they won't invent a new one. But I don't think we should bring both of them along with us. It would be too dangerous. One of them will be enough, if he pulls the stretcher like a wheelless cart. Which one do we take?")

("The big one?") said Firegold, indicating Hyrgis. ("If he understands me a little, I'd be able to give him orders if you were busy somewhere else.")

Aristeas looked at the two Arimaspians doubtfully. Hyrgis seemed much more intelligent than Skylas, and much more dangerous. On the other hand, because he was stupid, Skylas was also unpredictable and hard to control. He might decide to attack his captors without warning because he was hot or tired or because he was greedy for human flesh. And Firegold was right: It would be useful if the prisoner could understand what both his captors told him to do.

("Very well,") he agreed. ("Hyrgis it is.") He played a chord on his lyre, and the two Arimaspians blinked, sat up straight, and began glaring again.

("We'd better set off,") said Firegold. ("It will take more than a day for you to travel to the hunting party on foot, so we should start as soon as we can. We could travel for a few hours yet before it gets dark.")

("Very well,") Aristeas agreed—reluctantly, because he'd wanted to let his tunic dry properly before going on. ("Umm, why don't you go up and see if you can find the best route for me to take? I'll arrange the stretcher.")

Firegold at once took off like a partridge with a thunderous burst of wings and soared up into the afternoon sky. Aristeas went back into the dip and started packing his saddlebags. After a moment's thought, he took his clean tunic off and packed it, and put the wet one on. It would never dry otherwise. He began sorting out an Arimaspian pack that could be carried by Hyrgis.

"Human," called Hyrgis suddenly, "I'm thirsty."

Are you, by Zeus! thought Aristeas. He went on packing. He put the remaining mutton in the Arimaspian pack.

"Won't you give me some water?" asked Hyrgis. "You said you wouldn't let us die."

Aristeas tossed his saddlebags over his shoulders and

came up the slope, dragging the pack for Hyrgis. "I won't let you die," he said. "I want you to carry this."

"I need a drink of water first," said Hyrgis.

"Very well." Aristeas took out the water flask and stepped between the two prisoners to give it to Hyrgis.

Skylas lashed out almost at once. He rolled backward onto his shoulders and kicked madly with both legs. But Aristeas had been waiting for him and jumped out of the way. The force of the kick into empty air carried the Arimaspian on, and with a loud bellow, Skylas rolled a short distance down the slope and stuck firmly on a small hillock.

"Tch, tch," said Aristeas. "Here's your water, Hyrgis."

"Ow!" howled Skylas. "Ow, ow, ow! I'm on top of an ants' nest!"

Aristeas went and had a look. "So you are. Did you want some water, too?"

Skylas just wailed. Aristeas sang a quick spell over him, then went back up the slope and untied Hyrgis's feet. "Come along," he said. "We're taking you to pull the stretcher. Stand up; I need to fasten this pack on you."

Hyrgis stood up, looking at Aristeas with loathing.

"What about me?" howled Skylas.

"You can stay here," replied Aristeas. "I just fixed the spell on the ropes that hold you so that it will break at noon tomorrow, and after that you can make your own way home."

"Noon tomorrow?" cried Skylas. "The ants will have eaten me alive by then!"

"Of course they won't!" Aristeas told him. "They're wood ants. They'll bite you only if you annoy them by moving too much. Now, as my people say, much rejoicing! I hope I never see you again. Come on, Hyrgis. Do I have to cast another spell on you to make you walk?"

A few minutes later he was setting out eastward. Hyrgis walked in front of him, carrying the pack and pulling the stretcher with Wing-shadow's body on it, and Firegold, his wings gleaming in the afternoon light, glided back and forth ahead of them, occasionally drifting back to call down directions. It was, Aristeas thought smugly, not a bad way to travel.

Two days later he'd changed his mind. It was a dreadful way to travel. A griffin was a terrible judge of the best route for a man on foot. Firegold had directed the party up rocky mountainsides, down stony slopes, through tangled thickets of the dark-leaved bushes, across bogs—which looked like solid ground from the air—and through freezing mountain streams. Aristeas had taught himself how to swear in flicker-talk. And now the griffin had led them to the top of a sheer cliff above a wooded river valley. Aristeas stood on the edge, looking down at the crags of slippery shale, the bushes with their twisted roots clinging desperately to the few patches of earth, and, far below, the river rushing whitely along a stony bed.

("Firegold!") he shouted.

The griffin glided down, landed on the cliff edge beside him, and folded his wings nervously. ("What's the matter now, Excellent?") he asked.

("How am I supposed to get down this?") Aristeas demanded.

Firegold glanced down the slope. ("But you can walk across the valley, can't you, Excellent?")

Aristeas sat down and hung his feet over the drop. ("Do you see that?") he said to the griffin, lifting one squelching muddy boot. ("You know what that is, you empty-headed nearsighted numskull? It's a foot. A foot. It's soaking wet from stamping through your bogs and streams, and it has blisters from plodding over your wretched mountainsides. It has five toes, no feathers, and it's no use at all for flying!")

Firegold glanced down the slope again. ("But you must cross here!") he said. ("That river there is the old boundary of our territory. It cuts right across the mountains from south to north. There's no way around it for several hours' flight in either direction. But this valley is the last big patch of woodland between here and the Shoulder of the World, and once we're across, we'll be safely away from the one-eyes. Once you've climbed the hills to the other side, I can fetch the hunting party, and we'll have help.")

("If the hunting party can come as far as the east edge of that valley, why can't it fly across to the west edge here?")

("I've told you,") said Firegold. ("They're youngsters. They've been sent to catch game on the edges of our territory, which they'll take back to the Shoulder of the World and store for the winter. But the one-eyes have often ambushed hunters from that valley. Ten years ago the First Ones decided that for safety's sake no one was to cross the boundary without permission. And youngsters, like the hunters, are supposed to stay at least an hour's flight to the east of it. They'll be nervous of coming even to the east side of the boundary, and I could never persuade them to cross the river. You must cross it yourself, Excellent. You're such a powerful magician; one little cliff won't stop you, will it?")

Aristeas sighed, and looked wearily down at the river far below. He supposed that he could lower himself from the top of the cliff if he had a very long rope. But the only bits of rope he had were the fragments tying Hyrgis and the stretcher, and anyway, he had never liked heights. He scowled at the cliff top around him, bare except for coarse grass and a few scrubby bushes. Grass. He knew a charm for making rope out of grass; it was one of the first proper spells he'd learned. It wouldn't make it any easier to go down the cliff, but it seemed he had no choice. Still scowling, he wrenched up a handful of grass and began knotting the blades together.

"The griffin thinks you can get us across here, does he?" asked Hyrgis. The Arimaspian had never admitted that he understood flicker-talk, but he was making less and less effort to pretend that he didn't.

Aristeas nodded. He started whistling.

Hyrgis glared with a hatred that had been growing more intense by the day. "Is that magic again?" he asked, looking at the grass chain. The green blades were thickening and lengthening even as they were knotted.

Aristeas nodded. He picked another handful of grass and kept on knotting and whistling.

Hyrgis sat down with a thump. "Even if you can make a rope out of grass," he said, glowering down at the river, "I can't let myself down it, pulling a stretcher, with my hands tied."

Aristeas stopped whistling for a moment, though he kept on knotting grass. ("Firegold,") he said, ("could you take the stretcher down to the foot of the cliff?")

("Taking it down is easy,") said Firegold. ("I just need to hold it and glide.") He hurried over and took the stretcher from Hyrgis and, a moment later, disappeared with it over the cliff. Aristeas began whistling again. Under his fingers the knotted grass turned quickly into a long green rope.

When he'd knotted grass until his fingers were sore,

and the rope was finally long enough, Aristeas tied one end around the trunk of a particularly strong bush, then, after calling Firegold to stand guard, tied the other end around Hyrgis's waist.

"Now," he told the Arimaspian, "I will untie your hands, and I'll lower you down the cliff on the rope. When you get to the bottom, I want you to stand still, wait, and not try any tricks. Firegold will be watching, and he'll stop you if you try to get away or do anything stupid to me while I'm climbing down."

Hyrgis gave him a poisonous look but didn't make any threatening move when Aristeas untied his hands, and when the rope had been looped about the bush, he went over the cliff quietly. Firegold took to the air again and watched him as he descended.

("He's down and standing quietly,") the griffin reported a little later. ("Now it's your turn, Excellent.")

Aristeas made a kind of sling from the leather rope that had tied Hyrgis's hands and looped it around the rope of grass so that it would slide along the rope when it was loose but hold when it was tightened. He went to the cliff edge and looked over again. Hyrgis was invisible in the woods below, but the rope stretched down and down as though it were tying earth and sky together. Aristeas swallowed and reluctantly lowered himself over the edge.

It was a very nasty descent. Once some loose shale crumbled under his foot, and he fell twenty feet before he managed to tighten the sling and stopped, swinging and turning in thin air. His hands were shaking as he let himself slip down to where he could again brace his feet against the cliff.

He was about two-thirds of the way down and working his way around an overhang of rock when the rope gave the most tremendous jerk. He grabbed the rock with both hands, his legs scrabbling for a hold, and the rope whizzed through the loop of sling and came rattling down on top of him in great coils, followed by the bush he'd tied it to. He was vaguely aware of Firegold shrieking and diving, but all his attention was used up in clinging to the overhang with all his strength. Kicking and struggling, he was just pulling himself up onto the jutting edge of the shale when the rope gave another jerk, and he was left hanging by his hands again. He realized that Hyrgis at the bottom was trying to pull him off. "O Apollo!" he groaned out loud. ("Firegold! Help!") He tried to shake the sling off before he was hauled down by it.

The rope gave another jerk, but this time not so hard. The sling slid away from him, and the rope, the sling and the bush still attached, went plummeting down to the bottom of the cliff. Aristeas clung panting to the loose rock of the overhang. It was flaking away under his fingers. ("Help!") he shouted again. ("Firegold!")

There was a thunder of wings beside him, and then the griffin's talons locked into his shoulders. Gritty dust flew up from the rock with the force of the air from the huge wings. The shale broke, and he began falling, but the wings pulled him upward. The trees below, dark pines and spring green birches, swung wildly for a moment, then steadied. With Firegold's wings fanning about him, he floated slowly downward through the treetops and landed gently on a patch of mossy bog.

Aristeas fell flat on his face, then got up quickly, as the ground was wet.

("The one-eye's escaping!") Firegold told him urgently. ("I attacked him when he started pulling down the rope, but I had to leave him to help you! Over there!")

The griffin leaped into the air again and disappeared above the trees, heading in the direction of the cliff, which could just be seen through the tree trunks.

Aristeas began by running in the same direction, then stopped himself. If he met the Arimaspian face-to-face, Hyrgis could kill him easily. He unlatched his bowcase, took the bow out, strung it, and selected an arrow. Then he ran parallel to the cliff. After a moment he heard a crackle in the undergrowth and stopped. There was Hyrgis, crawling through the bracken, trying to keep out of sight of the griffin in the air above. The Arimaspian looked up and saw Aristeas at almost the same moment Aristeas saw him. He gave a strangled roar of rage and jumped to his feet, grabbing a young birch tree. He tore the sapling up by the roots and rushed toward Aristeas, swinging it.

Aristeas took careful aim and shot. The arrow whizzed through the air and tore the outside of Hyrgis's loose boot; it cut straight through the leather and pinned the boot to the ground. Hyrgis tripped with a bellow, dropping his tree. There was a squawk from the sky, and then Firegold slipped through the branches and landed on top of the winded Arimaspian. He raked the bristling red head sideways with one claw and lifted his knife-edge of a beak.

("Stop!") Aristeas ordered sharply. ("We still need him to pull the stretcher.")

("Treacherous, murderous, false-breeze hider-in-the-bushes!") said Firegold furiously. But he got off Hyrgis. ("Very well, you one-eyed bit of rotten meat,") he said. ("Get up. Don't pretend you can't understand me! Go back to the stretcher, and let Excellent tie you up again. Make one false move, and I'll tear your eye out.")

Hyrgis did as he was told.

At the foot of the cliff Aristeas looked up at the crag

where he'd hung a few minutes before and shivered. ("Are there more cliffs on the other side of this valley?") he asked Firegold.

("No,") replied the griffin. ("Only hills.")

Aristeas nodded, and the griffin turned to spring into the air again.

("Firegold,") said Aristeas, and the griffin hesitated, looking back over his shoulder.

("Thank you for catching me so quickly,") Aristeas told him. ("I could have died.")

("I know!") said Firegold angrily. ("That miserable earth-crawler! When this journey's over, I'll . . .")

("You know you can't hurt him! But anyway, thank you. I'm sorry I was so unpleasant to you on the cliff top.")

("Oh, never mind that,") said Firegold, embarrassed. ("I made things difficult for you by wanting to bring Wing-shadow. But we're almost safe now. Just the river to cross and a few hills to climb, and then I can fetch the hunting party to help us.") He leaped upward, flapped his wings, and began circling the valley, looking for the best place to cross the river.

Aristeas looked wearily at Hyrgis. "Start walking," he ordered.

"Next time," said the Arimaspian, and started walking.

The Shoulder of the World

5

The next morning Aristeas was singing as he washed his clothes. The party had reached the hills to the east of the river, and Firegold had gone to fetch the hunters. Hyrgis was safely tied up, it was a warm and sunny spring day, and there'd been roast quail for breakfast.

Aristeas sang:

> Some barbarian boy is flaunting with joy
> The shield which I left behind,
> Shoved under a bush
> in a bit of a rush
> and abandoned, the fine thing, with
> sorrow.
> But since I survive,
> and I'm glad I'm alive,
> what do I care for the loss of the gear?
> I'll buy me a new one tomorrow!

"Is that more magic?" asked Hyrgis suspiciously. The song was in Greek, and he couldn't understand it.

"No," said Aristeas grandly. "That's poetry. Not mine, but I like it."

Hyrgis grunted. "What's it about?" he asked after a minute.

Aristeas felt happy enough to be talkative even to Hyrgis. He translated the song, into flicker-talk because that was easiest.

Hyrgis squinted. "It doesn't make any sense. What is this thing that was left under a bush?"

"A shield. Big oxhide and wood thing to protect yourself in battle. You hold it on your left arm. If you want to run away, you drop it because it's heavy and slows you down. That's what the song's about."

"It's a song about running away from a battle?"

"That's right."

"And you like it?"

"Why shouldn't I?"

"I wouldn't have thought you'd like songs about running away. You're running into a battle—and what's more, one that isn't even yours."

"Oh, be quiet!" said Aristeas in disgust. "Having failed to murder me, you're now going to try to talk me out of helping the griffins, are you?"

"Why should you help them?" asked Hyrgis. "They're not your own kind. I'm more human than Firegold. Why should I be a prisoner and your enemy, while he's your friend? You're a fool to trust him. What do you think he's going to do, once his friends are here to help him?"

"I think he's going to have them carry his mate's body and, with any luck, carry us as well. I'm looking forward to that. I've had more than enough of walking."

"You really are a fool then. You're handing yourself over to a flock of the most dangerous creatures on wings. Most likely they'll kill both of us, now that our usefulness is over."

"Oh, I see. You're really worried that *I'm* going to kill you now that *your* usefulness is over. I don't know much about griffins, it's true, but I think what I do know, about Firegold and about you, is enough to tell me that I'm safe with them, but I'd end up in a cooking pot with your people." Aristeas wrung out his trousers, whirled them around in the air, then draped them over a bush and began singing again.

"You want to go home very badly, don't you?" said Hyrgis.

"As one of our poets says, I long to see 'even the smoke arising from the fires in my homeland.' As soon as I've seen out your dear Colaxis, I'll be home in Proconnesus as fast as my feet can carry me."

"That soon, eh?" Hyrgis sneered. "That soon may be never, human. Colaxis is not a power to be seen off easily, even with the help of your dear, well-trusted griffin friends—and you know only one of them, and he isn't even one of their rulers! You might or might not stop my queen, but it's likely to cost you your life and strength even if you succeed."

Aristeas stopped laughing.

"Why should you fight us?" Hyrgis went on, seeing that his listener was paying him full, though reluctant, attention. "My kind don't threaten your people. I've never even heard of these . . . Greeks—was it?—that you call yourselves. Your home is a world away, and when you talk about it, I can't understand half the words you use. We Arimaspians aren't going to try to take away from you things we've never even heard of! Why should you risk your life for the griffins? Or even the Issedones, if it comes to that? Why shouldn't you act like the fellow in your song and run?"

"Even if I were willing to abandon my friends," Aristeas said, after a moment of uncomfortable silence, "I couldn't. My master Apollo drove me here, and he won't let me go home until I've done what he wants."

"But Colaxis is very powerful," whispered Hyrgis. His eye was now gleaming very brightly. "She must know a potion that would deafen your ears to the god's orders."

"I can imagine the sort of potion Colaxis would give me," Aristeas said. "If I drank any brew of hers, the only place I'd go afterward would be the kingdom of the dead! No, thank you!"

"A clever magician like you could arrange some safeguard!" Hyrgis coaxed. "And I'm sure Colaxis would rather help you than fight you—though if she does fight you, I think she'd win. You'd be much better off if she helped you. Even if you do succeed in defeating her somehow, how can you be sure that this Apollo will let you go? He's just as likely to drive you to do something else, and you'll never get home."

"Hyrgis, be quiet!" Aristeas ordered angrily. "Just be quiet or I'll give you such a sore throat you won't be able to talk for a month!" He went back to the cooking pot and began scrubbing his tunic, hard.

He was relieved when a flock of eaglelike shapes appeared over the mountains eastward. He flung the washed tunic over a bush and hurriedly pulled on his clean one, trying hard to push from his mind everything Hyrgis had said.

The griffins circled above him once, then swooped, one after another. The rush and gleam as they fell toward him were beautiful and terrifying, and it cost him some effort to stand still, particularly after what Hyrgis had said. But when the griffins landed, they all bowed their heads respectfully. There were six "youngsters," and Aristeas was pleased to find that he had no trouble distinguishing them from Firegold. His friend was slightly larger and heavier than the younger griffins, and was a brighter shade of gold. Firegold had landed close to Aristeas, while the youngsters hung back, ruffling their feathers and rubbing their beaks against their wings nervously.

("Greetings,") Firegold said formally, lowering his head to his claws. ("Hunters, this is the magician Excellent, of whom I told you.")

("Greetings,") replied Aristeas politely. This caused more feather ruffling and anxious beak rubbing. The hunters had apparently found it hard to believe that a human really could talk to them.

("They've agreed to help us back to the Shoulder of the World,") Firegold said. ("West Wind and I can carry the stretcher with Wing-shadow, and Swiftbright and Lightningclaw thought they could carry you. They've brought some of the slings they had for carrying meat back to the Shoulder of the World, and you could ride in one.")

("Very good!") said Aristeas with more confidence than he felt. He noticed the slings now—a couple of animal skins woven together into a sort of hammock, attached to the griffins by straps like the twigs propping up a bird's nest. He didn't like the thought of thundering through the air in a flimsy thing like that. But he didn't like the thought of walking "four days' flying" into the high mountains, either—not after the two weary days it had taken him to cover "four hours' flying" on foot. ("What about Hyrgis?") he asked.

Firegold's crest feathers went up. ("Can't you tie him up with ropes that break the next day, the way you did the smaller one?")

("I don't think that would be wise,") Aristeas returned. ("Remember, he's understood at least part of everything we've said. He could probably tell Colaxis things that would be very useful to her.")

Firegold lashed his tail with excitement, and his eyes lit up. ("Good!") he exclaimed fiercely. ("He killed Wing-shadow, and I'm glad he won't go free! Release him first, please, Excellent. I don't like to kill an enemy who's tied up. Release him and let him run, and I will strike the murderer down!")

("By Apollo!") Aristeas exclaimed, exasperated. ("Haven't you understood anything I've told you? I captured him by magic, so he's under the god's protection. We can't kill him. We'll have to keep him a prisoner until it's safe to release him.")

("You can't kill him, but couldn't I?") pleaded Firegold.

("If you want me to ignore the god, I'll be off to Proconnesus now!") Aristeas told him. ("I've come here only out of obedience to the god's command. Hyrgis isn't my prisoner; he's Apollo's—your Lightning-flash's. It would be nice if Apollo 'came like night' and shot him dead, but I don't imagine the god will do anything so helpful, and if he won't, we can't. Your friends will have to carry him.")

("He looks very heavy!") protested one of the young griffins.

("Too heavy for two of us to carry,") agreed another, ("and the slings won't adjust to being carried by three.")

("Then I'll cast a spell that will make both of us lighter,") Aristeas said impatiently.

("You said you couldn't do that!") exclaimed Firegold.

("I couldn't do it to Wing-shadow's body!") corrected Aristeas. ("Enchanting Hyrgis is another matter entirely. He's not dead. Don't you understand *anything* about magic?")

Firegold looked ruffled and annoyed but did not protest again, and when Aristeas brought out the lyre, he even seemed rather proud. He explained to the youngsters that Excellent always worked magic by means of beautiful music. The youngsters were impressed and, when the spell had been cast, more than impressed: awed. Firegold just looked smug, as though the magic were his own.

They were ready to set out. Hyrgis, sullen and silent, was loaded into one sling, and Aristeas sat down in the other, setting his saddlebags and bowcase in his lap and clutching the straps with both hands. Firegold and West Wind had the stretcher, and the remaining griffin was to scout the land ahead. At Firegold's command, all seven sprang into the air. The huge wings thundered; the fragile straps that held the slings strained till they creaked. Aristeas clutched them so tightly his hands went numb, and he closed his eyes.

When the wings stopped beating, he opened his eyes again and saw that the hillside was already far below. The two griffins who carried him were soaring upward. They flapped a few times, glided, flapped again. Higher and higher they rose. Looking back, Aristeas could see the wooded valley of the boundary and the cliff where he had clung the day before, now small with distance. Before him rose the mountains, purple and silver in the sun. The wind was cold in his face.

He lay back in the sling and stared straight up at the sky. Unwillingly he thought again of what Hyrgis had said. Griffins were dangerous. He might never go home.

"O Apollo!" he whispered. "I wish I'd never asked you for anything!"

They flew all day, and the land below them grew steeper and rockier by the hour. In the evening, when the setting sun behind them was painting the peaks rose-pink, they descended at last. Aristeas was frozen from the cold wind and stiff from sitting tensely in the sling. He was in a bad temper, which was not improved by the bump he got when the griffins landed and was made even worse when he realized that the chosen campsite had no trees or bushes and thus no wood to make a fire.

("Firegold!") he called angrily, glancing around.

One of the other griffins—Lightningclaw, he thought it was, a smallish, sandy-colored she-griffin—timidly informed him that Firegold and West Wind were taking the stretcher up to the top of the nearest mountain peak, where the cold would preserve the body. ("But we'd be honored to help with anything you want, Excellent,") she told him. ("Firegold's explained what you're doing for us, how you're going to defeat the one-eye witch-queen, and we're all very grateful to you. Would you like some food? Sunstrike, who flew ahead of us, has killed a wild goat. You can have first choice of the meat.")

Aristeas groaned. ("I need something to build a fire with,") he said.

("Why?") asked Lightningclaw in surprise.

("To cook with! I can't eat wild goat raw!")

("You mean, you burn your food?") asked the griffin Swiftbright, as horrified as Firegold had been.

Aristeas scowled. He stamped into the dusk, nearly fell off a cliff, and finally found one scraggly bush of dry heather. He built a fire with it and enchanted it so it would burn long enough for him to cook on it. It seemed a great deal of effort for a bit of scorched goat meat.

("Firegold,") he said when the griffin reappeared, ("did you choose this campsite?")

("Yes,") said Firegold nervously. ("Don't you like it?")

Aristeas kicked at the stony ground. ("No wood for a fire, freezing cold rocks to sleep on, cliffs on two sides of it, no water, and a wind like a Thracian winter. By Apollo! What am I supposed to like about it?")

("But it's a very good place to camp!") protested West Wind, who was at Firegold's side. ("The wind is good and steady and makes it easy to land and take off, and the cliffs make it safe. The stones are clean to roost on, and as for water, there's some right at the cliff foot.")

Hyrgis gave a croak of laughter. "You see?" he said. "Griffins don't have the same ideas about what's good as we do, even when it comes to choosing a place to stop for the night. How can you expect to be their ally in a war? Our kind at least understands the use of fire and shelter."

"You be quiet!" shouted Aristeas.

("We'll have a more comfortable place to roost tomorrow,") said Firegold soothingly. ("Tomorrow night we can stay in a nice dry cave belonging to some friends of mine. And tonight we'll all sleep around you, and that will keep you warm.")

Rather sullenly Aristeas agreed.

The next day's flying was happier. Aristeas made an effort to talk to the griffins who were carrying him. Swiftbright and Lightningclaw seemed in awe of him and had been too shy to speak unless they were spoken to, but when he asked questions, they were soon interrupting each other eagerly with their answers. He discovered that home for all the griffins was a complex of caves that was called something that seemed to mean Strong Place, or Fortress. It was in the middle of the great ridge of mountains called the Shoulder of the World. There they assembled every winter, and there all griffin cubs were born. In the spring, though, the griffins scattered for hundreds of miles over the mountains, looking for game. Families usually went off to their own particular territory near the Shoulder of the World, but unmated youngsters, like Swiftbright and Lightningclaw, were sent in groups to hunt outlying regions. All the griffins hunted through the summer, and carried any game they didn't need at once up to a mountaintop, where it froze. In the autumn they spent several weeks ferrying it all back to the Shoulder of the World, where it was stored in ice caves and eaten over the winter months, when the bitter cold and howling mountain storms made hunting impossible.

About three thousand griffins, including cubs and elders, wintered at the Fortress, but only their rulers, the First Ones, lived there all year round.

("We all choose who the First Ones are,") Lightningclaw explained proudly. ("If someone's done something especially brave or wise, all the adults meet, and we vote on whether he or she should be a First One. I'm sure that must be very different from the way you humans do things. You all have queens, don't you? Two-eyes or one-eyes, humans have queens, like bees; that's what they say.")

("We Greeks don't,") replied Aristeas sharply. ("In fact, in Proconnesus we have a system of government a lot like yours. An assembly of the people, and a council that they appoint.")

("Really?") asked Swiftbright. ("Your kind of two-eye must be much cleverer than the the kind we have near here, Excellent.")

("We Greeks,") Aristeas declared smugly, ("are the cleverest people in the entire world.")

("Even cleverer than the beyond-the-wind ones?") asked Lightningclaw, deeply impressed.

("I don't know about them,") Aristeas admitted. ("I've never met them. But we're much cleverer than any of the people I have met. So, how many First Ones are there? And how long do they stay First Ones?")

But that, it seemed, was a confusing question. The griffins regarded becoming a First One as something like becoming an adult: Once it had happened, it couldn't unhappen again, and you were a First One for life. There were presently four First Ones. One, the eldest, was a magician; there was always one griffin magician on this council. The others had all been chosen for their courage in the struggle against the Arimaspians. Most of them were she-griffins; like female hawks and eagles, they tended to be slightly bigger and fiercer than their brothers.

("Everyone thought Wing-shadow would be a First One someday,") Swiftbright said sadly. ("She was so brave and daring. And they said she was the best scout flying.") He stared ahead to where Firegold and West Wind flapped onward with the stretcher.

("It's so sad,") agreed Lightningclaw. ("And poor Firegold! She'd only asked him to become her mate last winter. He was so proud and happy and so excited about setting out with her as her partner. And this is how they come home!")

("You take one mate for life?") asked Aristeas.

("Of course!") exclaimed the two together, surprised and a bit shocked at the idea of people *not* mating for life.

("Though when a mate dies,") said Lightningclaw, ("most people will eventually find another. I wonder if Firegold . . .")

("He's too old for you!") said Swiftbright very quickly.

Lightningclaw laughed. ("I wasn't thinking for *me*, downhead!")

Aristeas smiled. Listening to them talk, he could forget what Hyrgis had said about the griffins.

That night, as Firegold had promised, they stopped with a family of griffins who had a cave. The cave itself was dry, sheltered, and not uncomfortable, though the approach to it—a narrow ledge of rock in the middle of a sheer cliff—made Aristeas cover his eyes. The family—mother, father, two half-grown cubs—were absolutely amazed when Firegold introduced Aristeas. ("But, Mother, it can talk!") the younger griffin cub exclaimed.

("I can hear, too,") Aristeas told her, and the griffin cub dashed behind her mother and peered anxiously over the sleek back, her downy gold head feathers bristling like a dandelion.

What Aristeas actually had to say—that the Arimaspians had a plan to attack the griffins with bows—horrified the family.

("The whole people will have to hear this,") said the mother griffin grimly. ("Tomorrow, when you go, we'll fly, too. We'll go to our neighbors and start spreading the news to assemble at the Fortress.")

So they flew on the next day knowing that the country was being roused about them.

They continued on for the next two days into a land of rock and ice. Mountains rose on each side of them, and though they flapped their way along the lower slopes, the air was still cold enough to make Aristeas's hands quite numb, and he wrapped his blanket around himself inside the sling. At last, in the afternoon of the fourth day, they came to a huge ridge of peaks that stood out against all the other mountains. Firegold and West Wind, who were ahead of the others, shone against the dark flanks of the mountains like sparks from a bonfire.

("The Shoulder of the World!") cried Lightningclaw, beating quickly toward it. ("We're almost home!")

The wind boomed in Aristeas's ears. He rubbed his numb hands together and hoped that the Fortress was warm.

Lightningclaw and Swiftbright swooped downward and hovered for a moment above an outcropping of rock. Then, gently, they lowered the sling and settled beside it. Aristeas climbed to his feet, pulling his blanket over his shoulders. In front of him was a cleft in the rock about as wide as a man's height, and three times as tall. Firegold and West Wind with the stretcher already stood just inside it, and facing them was another griffin. It had the thinning feathers and hollow-eyed look of age, and it was white from beak to tail.

("That's Blizzard,") Lightningclaw told Aristeas in a very faint flicker-whisper. ("She's the oldest of the First Ones. She's the magician I was telling you about. And look! The rest of the First Ones are behind her. They must have assembled when Sunstrike arrived and said we were coming.")

Aristeas looked and saw that there were indeed three more griffins standing in the shadows behind Blizzard. He felt all at once horribly grubby and embarrassed and wished that he had put the blanket away.

("Greetings,") said Blizzard, stepping forward. ("Firegold, what is this?")

Firegold bowed his head to his claws, then braced himself and began to tell the First Ones everything that happened since he and Wing-shadow had first seen the one-eyes carrying Aristeas on the stretcher. The rest of the hunting party arrived with Hyrgis while he was speaking, but nobody else moved. When Firegold finished, Blizzard looked at Aristeas.

("I can see that you are a powerful magician,") she observed. ("More powerful than I have ever been. And you are called Excellent? Forgive us if we do not make you welcome all at once. Everything that Firegold has said about this one-eyed plot he has learned through you, from your questioning of the one-eyes in their own language. We do not see any reason why you would lie, but what do we know of you? Nothing. And no human, one-eyed or two-eyed, has ever before set foot in the Fortress. If we are to admit you and trust you, Excellent, we must know more about you.")

Aristeas bowed his head. ("That is reasonable. What do you need to know?")

There was a rustling among the other First Ones, as though they hadn't quite expected Aristeas to speak so well, but Blizzard didn't blink. ("They may have told you that I have a little magic of my own,") she said. ("If you want me to trust you, come here, and permit me to use it on you.")

Aristeas didn't move. The thought of walking into the shadowy cave and placing himself in the power of a griffin magician made him feel absolutely sick. Whatever had happened before, he had always had at the back of his mind a belief that his magic would help him, that through it he could always get the better of ordinary unmagical mortals. He glanced behind him at the rest of the hunting party and found Hyrgis's red eye watching him unblinkingly. The Arimaspian was grinning. Oh, Zeus! he thought wildly, I should have listened to him. I should never have come here. I'm trapped. If I don't let that old white griffin cast a spell on me, they'll kill me, and if I do let her, they'll still kill me.

("Are you afraid?") asked Blizzard.

Aristeas looked back at her. ("Yes,") he answered flatly.

Blizzard was silent. One of the other First Ones came up behind her and flickered something in a whisper. Blizzard flickered faintly back. The other griffin stepped forward. This one was a thickset powerful she-griffin, terribly scarred about the neck. ("If you do not agree to this,") she said, ("we cannot admit you.")

("And what will happen then?") asked Aristeas.

Both First Ones looked surprised. ("Then you must go back,") said the scarred griffin. ("Our people will take you to the boundary.")

("Oh!") said Aristeas, feeling weak with relief and a bit ridiculous. ("Is that all?") He hesitated. ("Apollo has sent me here,") he said at last. ("I cannot go back. I am bound to obey, as I hope you also are bound to honor the god.") He walked slowly and rather unsteadily forward and kneeled in front of the white griffin. Her eyes were a deep, clear red. She turned her head and fixed him with one eye, and it seemed to him that the depths flickered with a language of their own. He knew at once that she was casting a spell on him, casting it in her own way, but he remained kneeling, looking into the red depths, and did not fight. It was the most difficult thing he had ever done. After a little while he felt as though the eye had swallowed him up and he were standing in a red cave, his mind numb.

("Is what you told Firegold true?") asked Blizzard. Her voice seemed to flicker all around him.

He listened to himself answering without willing himself to speak. ("Everything I told Firegold is true.")

("And you believe you have been sent to us by this god whom you call Apollo?")

("Yes.")

There was silence, and the red lights flickered around him as though they were shining through water. ("There is a place in your mind,") said Blizzard. ("A place with trees of white stone, surrounded by water that glitters in the light.")

("That is Proconnesus, my home.")

("And you long very much to return there.")

("More than anything in the world.")

("And that is why you are angry with the god you serve? Because you wish to be there and he sent you instead to help us?")

("Yes.")

("And you fear us and wish in your heart to be rid of the burden of serving him.")

("Yes. But I have still come, Blizzard. I will do what I must. I asked Apollo for one gift, and he answered me with several that I had not asked for. I cannot give them back, so I must use them as well as I can, as you must.")

("As I will,") said Blizzard. The red light went suddenly black, and Aristeas again found himself kneeling on the floor of the cleft in front of the old white griffin. He took a deep breath and leaned back on his heels.

("Welcome to the Fortress,") said Blizzard, and he could have sworn she was smiling.

The Fortress

6

The Fortress turned out to be a much more wonderful place than Aristeas had ever expected.

To begin with, it was big. Once the First Ones had accepted him, they all escorted him in. Firegold flickered something about carrying Wing-shadow's body up to the snows, but Blizzard asked him to let West Wind and Swiftbright take care of that and to come along. Hyrgis was settled in a small side cavern near the entrance, under guard, and Aristeas was led down a long passageway. Cracks in the rocks let down occasional trickles of sunlight that were enough for him to find his way, but it was dark and full of the scent of feathers and dusty stone. He was glad that Firegold was walking beside him—or rather, half slinking, half hopping beside him, as griffins did on the ground. It was good to have one familiar shape nearby. He rested one hand on the griffin's smooth, warm neck feathers to reassure himself. Firegold looked up at him sideways but said nothing.

There was a peculiar hot, metallic smell in the passage now, and it was almost completely dark. Blizzard ahead of him showed white and ghostly, but the other First Ones were invisible in the blackness.

Suddenly the passage twisted, and he stopped, blinking, in a burst of golden light.

The First Ones walked on into an enormous cavern. Light coming through cracks at one side poured down onto a sheet of polished gold, which reflected it back to golden mirrors on the walls, so that the whole huge space was radiant. Everything in the cavern seemed to be made of gold. There were pebbles of gold-veined quartz scattered about the floor and heaps of gold dust in the corners. Gold dripped in huge icicles from the roof or formed columns with gold-covered pillars that rose from the floor. In the center of the cavern was a kind of well shimmering with the heat of a fire.

The First Ones went over to the fire pit and jumped up onto four boulders of gold-shot quartz. ("Again, welcome!") said Blizzard.

("He's staring at our gold like a thief!") protested the scarred she-griffin, turning her head to glare at Aristeas, who was still standing in the passage, gaping.

("Calm down, Avalanche!") an elegant pale gold First One told her. ("It's the one-eyes who always want to steal our gold, and this magician is helping us against them. I am called Driftfeather, Excellent; welcome!")

("I suppose we're bound to believe he's doing us a great service,") a small dark male First One said, though grudgingly. ("Blizzard has vouched for his honesty. I am Nightfall, human; welcome!")

("Please excuse my staring,") Aristeas said, recovering from his surprise and walking over to the fire well. ("I'd heard you hoarded gold, but I never imagined you had anything so magnificent.")

Even scarred Avalanche seemed pleased with the compliment. ("This is our assembly hall,") Blizzard explained. ("It's the heart of the Fortress. Gold is sacred to us, and we keep some of it all over our Fortress, but most is stored here. We use it in the worship of the gods and to make mirrors to spread the light. We don't know how to work any other metals.") The image of *working metal* was of beating a nugget with a rock held in the beak. Only a metal as soft as gold could possibly be worked that way.

("This is the middle of the Fortress,") Blizzard went on. ("Most of the other passages lead here. I'll show you the parts where we live next, and you can make yourself comfortable for the night. In the morning we'll have a meeting and discuss what to do.") She jumped off her boulder and led Aristeas across the assembly hall to a passage on one side of it. The other three First Ones remained where they were and began discussing one-eyes and bows anxiously among themselves. They called Firegold over to them, and as Aristeas left, he heard his friend starting to answer questions about everything that had happened.

Aristeas had never imagined that there was so much gold in the entire world. There were panels of it everywhere, reflecting the light down the narrow passageways and into little gold-walled side caverns that the griffins used as sleeping rooms. Gold balls and lumps of crystal swung by uneven leather strings from the ceilings of a few rooms, and crude gold basins stood in corners. All the rooms were empty. At this season the Fortress was occupied only by the First Ones, though Blizzard told him that more griffins would soon arrive for the assembly. Aristeas just nodded, staring at it all. He was so astonished that it took him some time to realize that he was feeling hot in his cloak and blanket and to wonder why the Fortress was so warm.

("There's a fire in the earth below the mountain,") Blizzard explained when he asked her, ("and it heats the water that comes from the rocks here. I'll show you.") She led him down another passageway. Aristeas folded the blanket over his arm and loosened his cloak as the air grew still warmer.

They came out into another large cave walled with gold mirrors. At the far side of it, a brilliantly blue spring splashed steaming from a crack in the rocks and flowed into a series of shallow ponds on the floor, before vanishing again into the stone. The air had a strong mineral smell.

("The water isn't good to drink,") said Blizzard. ("It's too full of salts. We use another spring in the upper part of the Fortress for drinking water. But this hot spring runs under most of the Fortress and keeps it warm, even in the coldest winter, and the water is very healthy for bathing in.")

("You bathe in it?") asked Aristeas, eyeing the warm blue pools eagerly.

("The one farthest from us is too hot, but yes, we bathe in the others.")

A blissful smile spread across Aristeas's face. ("A hot bath!") he exclaimed. ("You can keep your gold; just give me an hour or two in that water.") He gave a deep, contented sigh. ("This place will do nicely.")

A couple of hours later he trudged contentedly from the hot springs to the cave he'd chosen to sleep in and found Firegold sitting waiting for him.

("The First Ones want me to stay with you,") said Firegold.

("To protect me? Or to stop me from stealing things?") asked Aristeas—but without resentment. He was much too comfortable to feel annoyed about anything.

("Both, I think,") said Firegold. He turned his head to study Aristeas closely. ("You've taken off the skin you wear on your bottom half!") he said.

("Trousers,") declared Aristeas, ("are barbaric. In Proconnesus I'd be ashamed to be seen in them. I had to have some for the journey, particularly for riding horses in cold weather, but I don't have to wear them now, so I'm not. This tunic is a bit worn, but at least it's civilized. I'm wearing civilized clothing for a—moderately—civilized place.") He looked at himself critically in the gold mirror, then pulled out his knife and began trimming his hair.

Firegold laughed. ("Why did you tell Blizzard you were afraid?") he asked.

("Because I was,") replied Aristeas.

Firegold was mystified. ("You? But you're always so—so sure of yourself.") The hesitation before he said "sure of yourself" made Aristeas suspect he'd thought of a less flattering term first: "arrogant," maybe, or just "conceited." He looked at the griffin disapprovingly, but Firegold was going on. ("Why should a powerful magician like you be afraid of the people you've come to help?")

("Because I'm one poor, miserable, defenseless Greek alone in a fortress with a whole flock of the most dangerous creatures on wings.")

("Defenseless!") exclaimed Firegold. ("Even without using magic, you shot well enough to pin down that one-eye's foot without scratching it.") He paused thoughtfully. ("You were shouting at that one-eye a lot over the last few days; was he telling you lies about us?")

("He did try to convince me not to trust griffins,") admitted Aristeas, ("but, as you can see, I didn't listen to him. Where is he, by the way?")

("Still in that cave near the entrance. The First Ones

don't want him any farther in. We've taken the ropes off his feet and given him some food. West Wind and Sunstrike are guarding him.")

("Good! The less I see of him, the better I'll like it. Well then, is there anything for supper?")

Aristeas went to sleep that night feeling happier than he had for some time and dreamed of Proconnesus. It was a wonderful dream to start off with. He hurried along the wide street from the city gate to the marketplace and paused among the columns of the porch in front of the row of shops—the white columns that Blizzard had called trees of stone. Everything was where it should be: the temple of Apollo facing him across the market square; the round council house, with its cluster of public notice boards to his left; the marble fountain, surrounded by the statues of gods and of eminent citizens, including several of Aristeas's own ancestors. He could even see the red tile roof of his own house down the side street to his right. Doves cooed on the roof above him, and there were swallows nesting under the eaves. He felt so happy that his feet scarcely seemed to touch the ground as he bounded out into the square.

Then everything went wrong. The citizens of Proconnesus stopped buying and selling and talking, and all turned to stare at him. They shouted; someone screamed. Men came running with spears—men Aristeas knew, with whom he'd gone to school. "Kallias!" Aristeas called to them. "Leontes! What are you doing? Don't you remember me?"

But they didn't seem to hear. They braced their spears, watching Aristeas with fear and hatred. Aristeas shook his head and started toward them, then stopped again. He looked down at his feet, and saw they had become claws, and that he had become a griffin. "No!" he cried, but realized as he spoke that his voice was silent, and the shout was only a flicker, which his friends could not hear. They raised their spears.

Aristeas woke up with a scream and sat bolt upright, shaking. It was pitch-black. He felt his face with his hands, then felt his hands with each other, and it was all right, he was still human.

("What's the matter?") asked Firegold sleepily, shifting beside him.

("Just a dream,") said Aristeas with relief. But he was still too frightened to sleep. He sat still for a minute, listening in the darkness. He could hear the hot spring splashing over the rocks at the end of the corridor, and it made him thirsty. ("I'm going to get a drink of water,") he told Firegold. ("The drinking water is in the upper part of the Fortress, is that right?")

("Just the other side of the assembly hall from here,") said Firegold. There was a ruffle of feathers as he settled to sleep again.

Aristeas went out into the corridor, barefoot, feeling his way. He found the assembly hall without difficulty; as Blizzard had said, most of the other passages led into it. It was dimly lit by the fire in the central well—a sacred fire, Blizzard had explained, that was kept burning at all times. Aristeas had cooked his supper on it. He'd walked halfway across the room without even glancing around when he heard a noise on his left, and he looked about and saw Hyrgis crouching by the wall.

The Arimaspian had his hands full of gold dust, and more gold stuffed down the front of his hide tunic. But he'd stopped his thieving and was looking at Aristeas with a horrible glow in his red eye, his yellow teeth bared in a grin. Aristeas stood frozen with surprise for a moment, then opened his mouth to shout.

At once Hyrgis moved, and Aristeas found himself blinded by a cloud of gold. He coughed, trying to beat the dust out of his eyes. Then Hyrgis himself followed the gold he'd hurled. Still blind and coughing from the dust, Aristeas found himself knocked to the pebbled floor, and the Arimaspian's hands closed around his throat.

"You can't sing now, can you?" the Arimaspian gloated in a whisper. "I came to look for you as soon as I escaped, but I'd decided to give it up; the place was too big, and I thought I'd never find you." Hyrgis's hands gripped so hard that Aristeas feared his neck would break even before he was strangled. Desperately he pulled at those hands with his own, but he could no more shift them than he could bend iron. ("Firegold!") he shouted frantically. ("Firegold! Anybody! Help!")

It was no use. The flickering shout was not loud enough to wake the griffins from their sleep, and Hyrgis thumped his head against the ground. Aristeas tried to gasp but only choked. His head was swimming, and he knew that in another moment he'd lose consciousness. He pulled at the hands again, found a little finger, and bent it back with all his strength. Hyrgis roared in pain as the bone snapped. He stopped strangling and thumped Aristeas's head again. Aristeas struggled, gasped in one breath of air, and screamed as loud as he could. Hyrgis swore, and his hands tightened again. Aristeas fumbled at them, but his hands were numb, and everything, even the fear, faded away.

The next thing he knew, he was lying, gasping, on the pebbles, and his throat was hurting as though he'd swallowed burning pitch. He lay still with his eyes closed and tried very hard not to cough.

After a minute there was a rush of wings beside him, and then a griffin's beak stroked his throat. ("Are you all right now, Excellent?") asked Firegold anxiously.

("No,") answered Aristeas.

("Sunstrike is dead,") came another griffin's voice. ("West Wind said she left him guarding the one-eye while she slept. The one-eye must have tricked him somehow.")

("Tricked him and murdered him!") said yet another voice, one that Aristeas recognized as belonging to the scarred First One, Avalanche. ("And nearly killed our magician as well. Firegold! You were supposed to stay with him!")

("Excellent only got up to get a drink of water,") said Firegold miserably. ("I never thought I had to escort him for that! I thought the one-eye was safely under guard. Everyone did.")

("Where is Hyrgis?") asked Aristeas. He didn't move, even to open his eyes, and he was very glad he didn't have to use his throat to speak flicker-talk.

("He's escaped,") answered Firegold, still more miserably. ("I heard him shout, and then I heard you scream, and I came, and he left you and ran. I stopped to see if I could help you, and he got away.")

("Got away where?")

("Out of the Fortress. West Wind and the others are searching the cliffs for him outside, but it's a dark night, and if he got down the first crag, he'd be able to hide among the rocks. We'll catch him in the morning, though, I hope.")

Somehow Aristeas rather doubted that they would. He opened his eyes and saw Firegold's beak about an inch from his nose. He hadn't realized that a griffin could look so anxious. ("When he goes to Colaxis now,") he told Firegold bitterly, ("he won't only be able to tell her what we talked about; he'll be able to guide her straight to the Fortress, tell her what it's like inside, and show her a couple of handfuls of gold to convince her he's telling the truth. And you say he killed poor Sunstrike? I wish I'd let you at least *try* to kill him at the boundary.")

("You were honoring the god when you spared him,") said Blizzard. ("Perhaps the god has some task for him.")

("Even if that's true, it's not comforting,") replied Aristeas. ("The kind of part Apollo has for him to play might well be one I'd prefer to have left out.") He felt his throat cautiously. It was still fearfully painful, and he suspected that Hyrgis had damaged something inside. And now his head was throbbing, too, where it had been thumped on the floor, and his eyes were stinging from the gold dust. ("Can you fetch my lyre?") he asked Firegold. ("I need to cure myself.")

Aristeas played himself back to his feet, then went and had another hot bath. After breakfast he felt almost restored, and when Lightningclaw bounded in to tell him that the First Ones were meeting and wanted him to join them, he felt able to go. He picked up his lyre and strode off to the assembly hall. Firegold, who was now determined not to let Aristeas out of his sight, stalked after him.

The First Ones were sitting on their boulders by the fire well, but they stood up when Aristeas came in.

("Greetings,") said Blizzard. ("I'm very glad to see you've recovered. I'm sorry to say that we still haven't caught your attacker. We searched for him as soon as it was light, but we couldn't find him. Please sit down.")

The First Ones began the meeting by going over what they knew. Colaxis had at least a hundred magic bows already and expected to have more at the time of her planned attack, in another month. She was presently camped at a lake on the edge of the grasslands, four days' walk north of where Firegold had met Aristeas. The whole tribe of griffins was beginning to assemble; a few had arrived already that morning, and more were expected throughout the day.

("The conclusion I draw from all this is that we must attack as soon as possible,") said Avalanche forcefully. ("The longer we wait, the more weapons our enemies will have to use against us. If they're camped near open water and grasslands, they won't have as much protection from the woodland as they usually do. As soon as we've assembled, we should carry the war to them. I'd suggest a night attack.")

("I'm not so sure that we should attack at all!") said the small dark griffin, Nightfall. He was the only male griffin among the First Ones. ("They were camped there when the big one-eye left them, and he expected to report back there, but the witch-queen may have changed her plans.")

("Why would she do that?") asked Avalanche impatiently. ("She'd speed things up if she'd heard what the big one-eye has to say, but he won't have reached her yet. Even if we don't catch him, it will take him a long time to get back to his people on foot. All the more reason to attack soon, before he can!")

("There was another one-eye, though, who may have reached her already,") said Nightfall. ("Or so you and Firegold have said, Excellent.")

("Skylas,") agreed Aristeas. ("Yes, I should think he'd reach her about now.")

("What could he tell her?") asked Driftfeather.

Aristeas thought for a moment, then sighed. ("He could tell her that he and Hyrgis captured a human magician, who escaped, questioned them under enchantment, and went off with a griffin. That, I should think, is enough for her to guess that you now know what her plans are, which should be enough to make her change them. I'm sorry. I should have found some way to kill both of them.")

Avalanche appeared to agree. Blizzard, as before, said, ("You were obeying the god who sent you here when you spared them.")

Aristeas sighed again. ("Every time Apollo has anything to do with the problem, it gets more complicated.")

("Well, what does he want?") asked Blizzard reasonably. ("Why did he send you? It seems to me that we ought to try to answer that question before we start planning attacks.")

("Does it? Lightning-flash!") said Avalanche. ("It seems to *me* that we ought to worry about attacks now and gods later. I still favor an immediate attack, but it would be good if we could learn something more about what the witch-queen is planning now. Blizzard, you did have a spell that let you watch the one-eyes, only it wasn't much use, because no one knew how they were communicating with one another. But if you did it now, with Excellent here to interpret for us, we might learn something useful.")

("I'll do it,") said Blizzard. ("Though I still think we ought to consider the other question sometime, Avalanche. I'm sure it's important. Excellent, could you help me with this? It's a spell for seeing what's far off; perhaps you've done something similar before.")

Blizzard explained the spell to Aristeas as they went to her room to fetch some supplies. Aristeas had indeed done

something similar on occasion, but this sounded more powerful than the enchantment he'd used, and he was extremely interested. He didn't often have the chance to
discuss magic with another magician.

When they were back in the assembly hall, Blizzard
began the spell. She faced the fire well and prayed to Earth-
fire, who seemed to be a kind of griffin goddess, then
spread her wings and prayed to Lightning-flash. Driftfeather and Nightfall bowed their heads reverently, though
Avalanche ruffled her wings impatiently. Blizzard folded
her wings again, then brought out an image like a single
word: *fire*. But it was sung, rather than spoken, and so
powerful that the air seemed to tremble with it. Blizzard
walked slowly about the fire well, brushing its edge with
the tip of one white wing, the fire-image pulsing like the
beating of a heart. When the circle was complete, she stood
on her hind legs, grasped the rim of the fire well with her
claws and spread her wings to their immense full width.
Bracing herself, she swept the white pinions down, fanning
the fire. Ash flew from the coals, and they glowed, first
red, then orange, then yellow-white. ("Brightening!") she
called, singing the image so it dazzled behind the eye.
("Ember-fire brightens, whitens, air-shimmer holds!")
With the white glow holding all their minds, as well as the
fire, Blizzard nodded to Aristeas. He leaned forward over
the coals and sprinkled them with the perfumed dust they'd
gone to fetch and then with a handful of gold. Instantly
the fire well was filled with a thick white smoke.

("Show us the one-eyes,") commanded Blizzard.

The smoke twisted in the well, then formed into
shapes. Aristeas found himself staring into a face—an Arimaspian face, with its blind hollows and its single glaring
eye. He seemed to move back, and he saw that he was

staring at a woman. She was dressed in a gown of ti-
gerskin, fastened around the waist with a belt made from
gold beads and bits of bone, and over it she wore a long
cloak of a very white leather, with trailing fringes down
the front. Her long hair was dark red, almost bloodred, and
fell down her back from under a headdress made of a griffin's skull set in gold. He was suddenly certain that he was
looking at Colaxis, and he was taken aback: He had expected her to be older, uglier. This woman was horrible—all Arimaspians were that—but she was also
magnificent, even beautiful, and he guessed that she was
no older than he. Her mouth was moving as though she
were shouting at someone, but he could hear no sound.

Again he seemed to move back, and he saw at whom
Colaxis was shouting. In front of her was another Arimaspian, tied to a tree by a piece of horsehide wrapped around
him from feet to chin. His face was bruised and swollen,
and there was dried blood under his nose and at the corner
of his mouth. He was so battered that it took Aristeas a
moment to recognize him as Skylas. His mouth twisted,
and Aristeas guessed that he was whining something, but
still there was no sound. Blizzard's spell wasn't going to
bring words, Aristeas realized, because words to a griffin
were images, not sounds.

Quietly he picked up his lyre and played a phrase of
music, trying to work his own spell into the one Blizzard
had cast. He played another phrase, then a chord, and suddenly, the shouting seemed to explode from the fire well.

". . . dare you tell me you don't know!" shouted
Colaxis.

"But, Queen, I *have* told you!" protested Skylas. "I've
told you everything that happened! I couldn't understand
what he said to the griffin; it was just hot lights to me.
And they took Hyrgis with them."

Aristeas hurriedly began to translate for the griffins.

"I wish they'd left you in pieces!" Colaxis yelled viciously. "Hyrgis was a good scout. He'd have more to tell me than just that this magician cast a spell and went off with a griffin! You fool!" She slapped Skylas across the face.

Skylas began to snivel. Colaxis turned away from him in disgust, then pushed a lock of hair back under her headdress and turned back.

"We'll go over this again," she said. "What was this magician's name?"

"I don't know!" wailed Skylas. "Please, Colaxis, let me go! I haven't eaten for three days, and I'm perishing of thirst. I—"

"You stay here until you either tell me something useful or die!" hissed Colaxis. "You say you didn't even ask this magician his name?"

"We didn't know he was a magician when we caught him," whined Skylas. "You don't ask the name of something you mean to eat."

"Idiot! Where was he from, then?"

"Pro—Pro-something-us."

"He didn't say whether he was an Ionian?"

"He never said that word, that Yonian, at all, I told you! He said he was a Greeb or a Greep, or something like that. He said his people lived a two-year journey away, to the southwest. But Hyrgis thought he was lying, and that really he came from . . . you know, beyond—"

"Be quiet."

Skylas sniveled quietly.

"And he cast a spell on you, and on Hyrgis?" asked Colaxis. "How?"

"He just sang. It put us to sleep. And it was the same when he healed the griffin. He made music. It was horrible."

"And the third time, the time you don't remember what he did? He sang then?"

"Nnnoo—that time he used the music-making thing."

"Music-making thing? What thing? You hog, that's the first time you've mentioned a music-making thing! What was it?"

"Don't hit me, please don't hit me! I didn't know it mattered! The thing had strings, like bowstrings, but lots of them. The magician pulled on them, and they made noises—dum, dum, like that."

"Huh! So it was a sort of wooden frame with strings stretched from one end to the other, was it?"

"Yes. And it had a thing at the bottom, to make them sound louder, a tortoiseshell—"

Colaxis gave a shrill scream of horror. "A tortoiseshell?" she asked. "You miserable stinking he-goat! Not a tortoiseshell!" She slapped Skylas, then grabbed his ears and twisted them. "There wasn't a tortoiseshell! Say there wasn't!"

"There wasn't, there wasn't!" howled Skylas.

"You liar!" Colaxis let go. She glared at Skylas for a moment, then turned and began walking off. Another Arimaspian in a white cloak hurried over to her and bowed his head; Aristeas noticed that he was carrying a bow over his back and a quiver of arrows at his side.

"Do we break camp today, then, Queen?" he asked.

"Yes," said Colaxis. "It's clear that this magician questioned Hyrgis and Skylas and has gone to tell the griffins that we plan to attack them. We dare not stay in such open country. We will have to march toward their own territory, keeping under the trees as much as possible, and then turn into the mountains to attack them. It's a pity; I'd hoped to have twice the number of bows to shoot them with. But what we have should be enough."

"I'll tell the people to pack the tents and prepare to march to the southeast," the other said. He bowed his head again and went off.

Colaxis walked on, slowly, through what was clearly an Arimaspian encampment. Tents of felt, painted with patterns in red and white, surrounded her, and many of the people were wearing white cloaks and carrying bows. They must be the bodyguards Hyrgis had spoken of. She came to one tent that was bigger than the others. Two skulls—one of a human, the other of a griffin—were set on posts before the door. Colaxis went into this and sat down on a chair made of bones, and as she sat down, the fringes of her cloak fluttered, and Aristeas suddenly saw that they were hands: The cloak had been made from human skin.

After a moment the queen got up again and went over to a huge chest of black wood. She unlocked it and lifted the lid, and Aristeas saw that it was full of caldrons, murky liquids in bottles of glass and bone, and boxes of herbs, some of which he recognized as magical. Colaxis pushed them all aside impatiently and took a small leather box from the very bottom of the chest. She opened it and pulled out its contents: a single sheet of rolled papyrus. Aristeas held his breath as she unrolled it—and saw the very last thing he had ever expected. It was written in Greek.

The Prophecy

7

("What is it?") flickered Avalanche in a whisper.

("Quiet!") ordered Aristeas, because Colaxis had begun to read the scroll. Aristeas, looking over her shoulder through the magic smoke, began to read aloud.

> "Go to the queen and give her this reply:
> You will hold wide lands beneath the
> northern sky.
> Your people all will tremble at your
> voice,
> and your heart victorious in power will
> rejoice,
> until the day when from Ionian shores
> comes one to force obedience to my laws.
> Then sealed eyes shall break in weeping
> springs
> when tortoiseshell with parting sorrow
> sings."

"O Lord Apollo!" said Aristeas, laughing in wonder, and added the Greek victory cheer *"Io Paian!"*

Colaxis jumped as though she'd heard him. She

clutched the scroll and looked around wildly. "Someone is spying on me!" she whispered. "Someone . . ." Her face set. "Is it you, magician? Then take that!" She reached into the black chest and seized a jar of carved bone, wrenched off the lid, and scattered the contents about her with a whirl of white cloak and red hair.

There was a crack like thunder, and from the well the fire shot up suddenly as high as the roof of the assembly hall. The watchers flung themselves backward. Aristeas's hair was singed, but the main force of the fire blast engulfed the magician who had cast the seeing spell—Blizzard. The white griffin was swallowed by a cloud of flame. She fell onto the pebbled floor, her beak gaping soundlessly in agony, and the fire from the well followed her, bending down as though it wanted to consume her. The hall was full of shrieks and frantic shouts for someone to fetch water. Aristeas seized his lyre and played three chords, and the seeing spell broke.

The fire sank down to the coals again, but it had done its work. Blizzard's plumage was burning. She screamed, rolling over and over on the floor, scattering fragments of burning feathers; there was a terrible smell. The First Ones scattered, some running to fetch water, others, led by Avalanche, trying to scrape gold dust and pebbles over their twisting, shrieking colleague to smother the fire. Aristeas tore his cloak off, threw it over Blizzard, and dropped on top of it. Blizzard screamed again and clawed at him wildly, then lay still, panting.

Aristeas climbed back to his feet and pulled his cloak off the other magician. The fire was out, and she lay limply, scarcely recognizable as a griffin. Her white feathers were scorched and blackened right down to the blistered skin. Nightfall and Driftfeather hurried up with gold basins of water in their beaks and began splashing it over her, and she shuddered weakly and gave a little chirrup of pain.

Aristeas picked up his lyre, sat down against the rim of the fire well, and began to play the healing spell yet again.

There was a long silence filled only by the cool sound of the lyre. When Aristeas had finished playing, Blizzard was the first to stir. She climbed to her feet, stretched one wing uncertainly, looked at it—and then, incredibly, laughed. ("Thank you, Excellent,") she said. ("That is a most marvelous spell. But do you know one for beauty?")

Looking at her, Aristeas saw what she meant. The spell had healed her burns, but many of her scorched feathers were still in place, sticking out through a new growth of fluffy white down. Black and white speckled and grimy all over, she was almost indescribably bedraggled. She was plainly feeling better, though.

("Don't thank me,") Aristeas protested, far less cheerful than she was. ("It was my fault you were burned. I shouldn't have shouted.")

("Excellent, the witch-queen might have realized we were watching at any moment. It's dangerous to use magic to spy on a witch. I knew that when I cast the spell. Still, it was worth it. What was the magic thing in the box?")

("The magic thing?")

("Yes, the bit of white bark or whatever it was, with the markings on it. You knew what it was as soon as you saw it. And you were overjoyed.")

("But didn't you understand?") asked Aristeas. ("That was a response from the Delphic oracle—a prophecy that promised victory in this contest to us!")

The First Ones didn't understand. They so thoroughly didn't understand that it was hard even to explain it to them. To begin with, they'd never heard of writing. He sent Firegold to fetch his saddlebags and showed them his own parchment book, and eventually they grasped the idea that words could be symbolized by markings, that the markings Colaxis had had were the sort used by Aristeas's own people, and that they were some kind of message.

("But *why* did the witch-queen have this message, and what did it mean?") Avalanche demanded irritably. ("Who sent it? And why were you so pleased about it?")

("One question at a time!") protested Aristeas. ("I've told you already, it was a response from the Delphic oracle.")

("The what?") asked Avalanche.

Aristeas ran his hands through his hair. ("The . . . oh, let me begin at the beginning. An oracle is a place or person used by the gods to speak to mortals. People can come to one or send a message, asking the god a question, and the god will answer them, usually through a priestess of some kind. The most famous oracle is at the temple of my master Apollo in Delphi, the navel of the earth, where the god killed the great earth serpent Python when the world was new. This temple is so famous that people come to it from all over the world. I've heard that even the Hyperboreans, the beyond-the-wind people, send offerings there, as well as to the god's birthplace at Delos. Colaxis must have heard about the oracle and sent to Delphi to learn how long she would rule. I suppose she wanted to be able to take precautions against her enemies. What we saw was the answer Apollo gave her.")

("How do you know?") asked Nightfall skeptically.

("I'd be a fine poet and servant of Apollo if I couldn't recognize the style of the Delphic oracle! Apollo always talks like that, in that kind of verse. I'm astonished that Colaxis could read it. She must have used magic to learn because, as far as I know, I'm the very first Greek to have come to this part of the world.")

("Then who carried the message here?") replied Nightfall.

("Oh, well . . . she could have given her question to an Issedonian, who gave it to a Scythian, and so on until it reached a Greek. That's how the beyond-the-wind people sent offerings to Delphi, according to what I've heard.")

Nightfall looked dissatisfied. ("I don't like it,") he said. ("It sounds to me as though the beyond-the-wind people might have something to do with this.")

("They've never helped the one-eyes, Nightfall,") said Driftfeather. ("And this isn't to the point. Excellent, what did this prophecy mean? You said it promised us victory, but I didn't understand it at all. How did it go? 'Go to the queen and give her this reply—' ")

("'You will hold wide lands beneath the northern sky,'") Aristeas said, translating as he quoted. He had a good memory for poetry. ("'Your people all will tremble at your voice, and your heart victorious in power will rejoice.' In other words, Colaxis will overcome her enemies within the tribe and rule the Arimaspians *until* 'the day when from Ionian shores comes one to force obedience to my laws. Then sealed eyes shall break in weeping springs when tortoiseshell with parting sorrow sings.'")

("And what does all *that* mean?") asked Nightfall.

("Apollo always talks in riddles,") said Aristeas. ("In fact, this oracle is clearer than most. Colaxis will rule until an Ionian—that's me—comes and forces the one-eyes to honor the decrees of the god, which at the moment they despise. He—that is, I—will succeed in doing this by means of a singing tortoiseshell. That isn't mysterious at all; any Greek would understand at once that it meant a lyre. The one-eyes will be defeated and weep.") He frowned. ("But Hyrgis said they can't. He said that long ago they had an ancestress who sealed up their eyes precisely so that they couldn't weep. I suppose the oracle just means that the one-eyes will grieve at their defeat.")

("Perhaps,") said Blizzard uncertainly. ("I still find it not very clear. And I thought you were . . . some other-sounding word, not the I-one.") Like all griffins, she couldn't manage any sound-names.

Aristeas grinned. ("So did Colaxis, didn't she? Skylas told her I was a Greek, and the prophecy said she had to fear an Ionian, so she thought she didn't have to worry. But if she'd known a bit more, she'd have realized that Ionians *are* Greeks—that part of the Greek people who are descended from Apollo's son Ion. We're the cleverest of the Greeks, just as the Greeks are the cleverest humans.")

("And the most modest as well,") said Blizzard dryly. ("But the witch-queen has realized now that the prophecy is coming true. She understood what the tortoiseshell meant.")

("Yes, that frightened her, didn't it? Until then she must have thought that if the god told her she'd rule until a tortoiseshell sang, she'd rule forever.")

("So she knows now that she's in deadly danger,") said Blizzard, completely serious. ("That's dangerous for us all, but particularly for you, Excellent. She'll do her utmost to kill you.")

("She can't cast a spell on *me*,") Aristeas said confidently. ("I'm much too good a magician for anyone to do that without my permission. And I don't see how else she can reach me, here in the Fortress. But I agree, we'd better take some precautions. No more seeing spells, for one thing. And some kind of clouding spell so she can't spy on us the way we spied on her, and some protective charms—")

("This prophecy business is all very encouraging,") interrupted Avalanche, ("but not as much use as you two magicians seem to think. We're still faced with an attack by one-eyes armed with bows, and we still haven't learned anything that will help us fight it off.")

("We have learned that the one-eyes are changing their plans, though,") said Nightfall.

("It's no use hoping to catch them in the open at the lakeside,") agreed Driftfeather. ("They'll be traveling under cover of the forest now until they're near the Shoulder of the World.")

("So we know we can't follow my first plan,") admitted Avalanche unhappily. ("But what plan can we follow? The one-eyes are going to be on their guard against us. They're starting off to attack us today, and, as you say, they'll stay in the woodland as long as they can. Probably most of them will stay in the woods, along with their flocks and herds, while the warriors march into the mountains. They have enough bowmen to destroy us with little risk to themselves if we try to attack them while they have the cover of the woods. We can do some damage to them when they enter the mountains, but even then, we're likely to suffer terrible losses. Any suggestions on how to stop them?")

Firegold, who'd watched silently since the meeting began, suddenly got to his feet. ("May I speak, First Ones?") he asked.

The First Ones looked at him in surprise. ("If you have a suggestion, youngster, come out with it!") said Avalanche.

Firegold's tail twitched at being called "youngster," but

he spoke in a humble tone. ("You all know how Excellent and I started back here, with Excellent walking and the one-eye pulling Wing-shadow's body on a stretcher. We traveled for two days like that, and it made me understand something I'd never really appreciated before.")

("What's that?") asked Avalanche.

("Humans can't fly,") replied Firegold. The First Ones gave flickers of amusement or impatience, and he went on quickly. ("We all know that, but we never think what it means. I kept directing Excellent through bogs and up and down steep hills, and he was very annoyed with me. The point I'm trying to make, First Ones, is that a human can't just walk anywhere a griffin can fly. An army of one-eyes marching from the woodlands to the Shoulder of the World will have to find a path they can use. Now, we know that one-eyes *can* reach the Shoulder of the World because we've fought them near here in the past, but we've never asked *how* they reached it, because there are so many ways *we* might have reached it that it wasn't worth considering. But in fact, if I remember rightly, the mountain ridge just north of here is so steep and craggy that it would be almost impossible for a human to cross, except at one point."

("Where the White River has cut across it in a ravine!") said Nightfall, beginning to get excited. ("You're right! I never thought of it, but the only way they can possibly attack us is by marching up that ravine!")

("And if we know they're going to come up the White River ravine,") said Firegold, ("we can prepare it for them.")

("Firegold,") said Avalanche, ("when Wing-shadow chose you for her mate, I thought it was a pity. Such a bold and daring young scout, I thought, throwing herself away on a fellow who, though undoubtedly fine to look at, is snow-silent and doe-hesitant. I take it all back. You'll be a First One someday. We can prepare the White River ravine so the one-eyes fall like sheep!")

("Like trees in an avalanche, you mean,") corrected Firegold slyly.

Avalanche laughed. ("I meant—but it was immodest to say so myself. Blizzard! Excellent! You two really are going to have to work on those precautions you were talking about. This ambush must be a surprise, and I don't want the witch-queen spying on it.")

Aristeas got tired of precautions over the next few days. The First Ones insisted that he have a griffin guard at all times, though in the end this usually wasn't Firegold, who was extremely busy organizing the ambush. Aristeas and Blizzard sang and flickered a clouding spell and a protective charm over the Fortress and the assembling army of griffins. The next day, though, Aristeas was aware of something wrong with his spells: The soundless musical hum they left had acquired a kind of whining buzz, like a mosquito trying to bite. Colaxis, he realized, was indeed trying to break them. He and Blizzard renewed the spells and then had to renew them again before the evening. They also went to the White River ravine and enchanted it as well. There was still no sign of Hyrgis.

When Aristeas got back to the Fortress afterward, he noticed that Blizzard, who'd flown with him to the ravine, was looking bedraggled and exhausted. ("You should rest,") he told her. He'd grown very fond of the old griffin.

("I've been finding it hard to,") confessed Blizzard. ("These are such troubling times.")

("I'll play for you.")

("Lightning-flash! I've only done half as much magic as you have during the past few days, and I'm exhausted. Aren't you tired at all?")

("I am tired. I was suggesting music, not magic.")

("!") said Blizzard. ("Thank you.")

They sat down in Blizzard's room, and Aristeas played the lyre. Blizzard lay with her head on her claws, listening. ("Excellent,") she said after a while, ("did you study fighting as well as music in your own country?")

("Of course I did,") he answered, playing on without a pause. ("All my people do—all the men, I mean. Greek women don't fight wars, though the women of some of the other tribes I've met do.")

("I thought you had, the way you were talking to Avalanche. Whom do your people fight?")

("Barbarians mostly—Scythians and other tribesmen who raid our land. Sometimes we fight Greeks from other cities. In Proconnesus we've never had any wars actually within the city, thank the gods, though some other cities have.")

("Wars within a city? You mean, as though griffins living in the Fortress were to kill each other? How horrible! Does that really happen? . . . Why?")

("Some people want a city to be ruled by an assembly of all the citizens,") he said, ("and some people—like my father—think it should be ruled only by the best—that is, the richest and noblest—families. And the two groups quarrel.") He bowed his head over the lyre and concentrated on his playing. He didn't want to say any more. He didn't like remembering the bitter arguments between the two forces in Proconnesus, and his father's rages over the other party's doings; he liked to think of Proconnesus as nearly perfect. But he remembered unhappily how shocked he'd been when he went back two years before and how much fiercer the argument had become. ("Why are you asking?") he said to Blizzard, to change the subject.

("I've been thinking about the prophecy,") she replied, ("and about why you were sent here. Excellent, I'm sure this battle Firegold and Avalanche are planning won't solve anything. We haven't yet answered the riddle of what your god intends.")

Aristeas stopped playing with a twanging of sour notes. ("Yes, we have!") he said angrily. ("Everything's perfectly clear. I was sent because it would take a powerful magician to stop Colaxis. I used the lyre when I enchanted Hyrgis and Skylas, and so I discovered her plans. I've told your people: You'll kill Colaxis in the ravine and destroy all the magic bows. Then things here in the north will be safe, and I can go home!")

("Did it need a magician as powerful as you to enchant two one-eyes with a truth-telling spell?") asked Blizzard. ("And why were you sent *here*? From what you've said, there were plenty of enemies closer to your home, plenty of other terrible wars that Lightning-flash might have sent you to stop, but didn't. And I don't think you have fulfilled the prophecy yet. It was when the tortoiseshell sang 'with parting sorrow' that the one-eyes would grieve, and what that means, we don't know. Besides, I've been thinking about what Nightfall said, and I think he's right. The be-yond-the-wind ones *do* have something to do with this; they helped Colaxis get that prophecy somehow. Excellent, what we need to do is go to them and ask them to help us.")

("Nobody knows how to reach them,") said Aristeas sullenly.

("That's not true,") said Blizzard. ("I know.")

("What? How? If you know how to reach them, then why haven't you?")

Blizzard was silent for a moment. ("I'm not a good

enough magician,") she said. ("And I'm old. I'm afraid that if I used . . . that magic . . . I might not come back.")

("Oh!") Aristeas looked at her fearfully. ("It's one of *those* spells, is it? The ones you have to stand on the edge of death to work.")

("Yes.")

He looked away. ("I think you're wrong,") he said. ("I think it's all been fulfilled already. It would be stupid to risk death when the whole thing will be over in a few days anyway.")

Blizzard turned her head and looked at him evenly, and he couldn't look back.

("If you like, I will do it myself,") said Blizzard. ("In fact, I should have done it already. It's selfish and cowardly of me to try to persuade you to go instead.")

("No!") he said in alarm. ("You're older than I am, you're not as powerful, and you're not well. You're quite right: Doing a spell like that would probably kill you, really kill you so you couldn't come back. No, you mustn't. If anyone's to go beyond the wind, it should be me. But I'm not going to do it now—not when there's a very good chance that the battle will settle everything and there's no need to go at all.") He stood and picked up his lyre.

Blizzard looked at him with such sadness in her red eyes that he suddenly bent over and stroked the burn-speckled neck feathers. ("You should rest,") he told her. ("Don't worry! It will be all right.")

The old griffin took a lock of his hair in her beak and preened it gently. ("Why is your race so savage when you can be so kind and create things that are so beautiful?") she asked. ("I'll try to rest.") And she seemed so grieved that he went away very thoughtful.

That night, when Firegold appeared in their sleeping room, Aristeas asked him whether there were any other tribes of griffins besides the one in the Fortress.

("Not now,") answered Firegold. He sat down and began preening his wing feathers. He was extremely pleased with his ambush, and he straightened his pinions with great satisfaction.

("But there used to be,") said Aristeas.

("Yes,") said Firegold, not paying much attention.

Aristeas watched him irritably. ("And humans killed them,") he said.

Firegold looked up. ("Have you only just realized that?") he asked. ("Yes, humans killed them. Some lived in the lower mountains westward, and one-eyes attacked their lairs and killed them for the gold. The rest lived out in the grasslands, and two-eyes shot them. I don't know why.")

("To protect their herds,") Aristeas said. ("I've seen pictures made by every people from the Issedones to the Scythians of griffins killing horses. The humans thought griffins were just wild animals, like tigers, and the griffins probably didn't understand that those horses had owners. The humans couldn't hear your language, and you couldn't understand theirs. I'm amazed now that your people trust me.")

("Oh, well,") said Firegold, embarrassed, ("you're different, aren't you, Excellent? I mean, you can talk our language. You're not like a human at all.")

Aristeas remembered his dream and groaned. ("All I want is to go home!") he said.

("Yes, we know that!") replied Firegold. ("Well, after the battle you can!")

The next few days passed quickly. Griffin scouts reported spotting the Arimaspians moving through the woodland to the north of the mountains, going east toward the Shoulder of the World. A couple of days later the main part of the tribe stopped in the forest, while the warriors turned south. They camped that night in the foothills of the mountains and were expected to reach the White River ravine about noon the following day.

Aristeas asked the griffins to take him to the ravine with them next morning. ("Colaxis may try to ensorcell you when you attack,") he said, ("and even if she doesn't, I can do some shooting.") So he, his lyre, and his bowcase were flown there, and he sat between Blizzard and Firegold and waited. Below him a cliff dropped sheer into a deep cleft in the mountains, cut by a river so white and woolly with rapids that from the air it looked like a flock of sheep.

There were about a thousand griffins with him—all the youngest and strongest members of the tribe. Avalanche explained the battle plan to them. They must not attack when they first saw the one-eyes, but wait, out of sight on top of the ravine, until the whole army had entered the ravine and couldn't escape. Then they could push onto them the rocks they had prepared. They were not to fly over the ravine, or they might be shot. When enough one-eyes were dead and Avalanche gave the signal, the griffins could fly down and attack the rest. They must be particularly sure to destroy all the bows and to kill Colaxis.

Shortly before noon a scout flew back and reported that the one-eyes were nearing the ravine, right on schedule. A ruffling and a flutter went through the griffin army, then subsided. Aristeas began to play his lyre to calm himself, until Avalanche told him to be quiet. He strung his bow instead and plunked on its string nervously until both Firegold and Blizzard begged him not to.

After what seemed years they heard the sound of feet skidding on the rocks far below, and after crawling to the edge of the cliff to peer cautiously down, Aristeas saw the vanguard of the Arimaspian army scrambling up the track beside the river, tall men and women in loose hide cloaks, carrying the long black club-sticks that Hyrgis and Skylas had used. It seemed to take hours for them to walk past; on the narrow track, they could walk only two or three abreast. He counted a hundred of them, and then began a file of men and women in white cloaks carrying bows. Colaxis's bodyguard. After twenty of them came a woman walking alone, gold gleaming on top of her long red hair.

("Do we attack?") Firegold asked Avalanche, in an eager whisper.

("Not yet!") said the old griffin. ("Half the army is still below the ravine. We've got plenty of rocks and people farther up the track to deal with these.")

Just then they heard a shout from farther up the ravine, an Arimaspian bellow. Below them Colaxis stopped. Then a figure came running down the ravine, pushing past the Arimaspian vanguard. Aristeas could just hear what he was shouting. "Queen!" he was yelling. "Queen, stop! It's a trap! You must go back!"

("It's Hyrgis!") he exclaimed. ("He knows we're here, and he's warning her!")

Avalanche understood at once and wasted no time. ("Attack!") she shouted. ("Loose the rocks *now*!")

As Colaxis hesitated and Hyrgis pushed his way toward her, the griffins pulled aside a tree trunk gate and sent a huge heap of rocks roaring from the cliff top. The Arimaspians all looked up and began screaming.

"Cover your heads!" Hyrgis bellowed, so loud they could hear him over the thunder of the rocks and the screaming of the army, "Cover your heads and go back!"

"Retreat!" screamed Colaxis as the rocks crashed into her bodyguard. "Retreat!"

With shrieks of excitement, the griffins began hurling the single stones from the cliff. Colaxis's army milled about helplessly. The files behind the bodyguard, too far away to hear the cries, were still marching forward, and those in front couldn't make them understand that they were to stop and hurry back. Hyrgis reached Colaxis, and Aristeas saw the two clearly for a minute, amid the chaos of falling stones and struggling, falling Arimaspians, standing together and speaking. Then a new pile of stones came thundering down, and Colaxis flung her white cloak about her head and began shoving her way brutally back down the path, with Hyrgis behind her. He'd got himself a new stick, and as one rock hurtled down toward him, he struck it aside. The whole army had turned around now, and was running back the way it had come.

("The boulders!") shouted Avalanche, ("Release them! Block off their retreat!")

The small stones propping the boulders on the cliff edge were knocked aside, and the great blocks of granite teetered for a moment, then came down with a sound like an earthquake. They tore through the Arimaspian army, leaving a trail of crushed bodies behind them, and landed in the river with a splash like a waterfall. But they missed Colaxis.

Aristeas selected an arrow, got to his knees on the cliff edge, and aimed carefully at the gold-spangled figure with the white muffled head running in front of Hyrgis. He prayed to Apollo and released the string.

Colaxis stumbled just as he shot, and the arrow whirred past her shoulder and skidded across the rocks. She looked back over her shoulder, and even over the distance between them, he could feel the fury and hatred in her eye. Then she kept running. He snatched up another arrow and shot again, but the range was growing too great for his bow; his arrow struck fairly into the cloak of human skin she was using to protect her head, but he could tell it hadn't penetrated deep enough to hurt her. He shot again, furiously, but she was out of range.

Rocks fell and boulders crashed farther down the ravine. Aristeas jumped to his feet and raced along the cliff top, looking for an opportunity to shoot and not finding one. The Arimaspians were getting away. Dead lay in numbers beside the river, many of them white-cloaked, some armed with bows—but not enough of them to cause more than a temporary upset to Colaxis's plans. Some of the griffins leaped into the air and began swooping down upon their enemies to attack them at close quarters, but at this the archers below stopped. The griffins on the cliff top had to stop hurling stones for fear of hurting their own people. The drop to the bottom of the gorge was long, and the archers were able to shoot several times while the griffins approached. Griffins fell, crashing into the cliffs or landing, struggling, in the white waters of the river and rolling over the rocks to lie drenched and sodden on the edges of the shallow stream.

("Halt, halt!") shouted Avalanche. ("Halt! Blackness! Lightning-flash! Let them go!")

And the remaining Arimaspians scrambled back out of the ravine to safety.

To Face Death Twice

8

The First Ones held another meeting that evening. A hundred and sixty-four Arimaspians lay dead in the White River ravine, of whom thirty-seven wore the white cloaks of Colaxis's guard. The griffins who had descended to the ravine, however, had recovered only twenty of the magic bows; the rest must have been taken from the dead by other Arimaspians and were still in enemy hands. The bodies of thirty-nine griffins had been gathered up from the ravine and now lay in the snows of the Shoulder of the World, waiting for a thunderstorm and burial in the lightning. Griffin scouts, flying high up out of bow shot, reported that the Arimaspian army had stopped for the night in the valley of the White River to the north of the ravine.

("But they'll have to come back to the ravine,") said Avalanche. ("As Firegold said, there's no other way they *can* come if they want to reach the Shoulder of the World. We'll defeat them yet!")

("What if they just go home for now?") asked Nightfall sourly. ("It's what I would do. Leave us, and go attack their two-eyed neighbors this autumn, then return next year by another route, with two-eyed bowmen as well as their own.")

("Why would the two-eyes help them?") asked Driftfeather.

("Why wouldn't they? If they've been conquered, and the one-eyes threaten to eat them if they don't and reward them if they do, why shouldn't they help the one-eyes kill us? They've been happy enough to kill griffins in the past for less reason.")

("If the enemy won't advance,") said Avalanche, ("we'll have to attack.")

("They still have at least eighty of those bows,") said Nightfall. ("Hundreds of us will die.")

West Wind, who'd been working as a scout, slid into the assembly hall. ("First Ones,") she said anxiously, ("the one-eyes are slicing up their cloaks and the firewood they brought, and chopping down bushes and—and making things.")

("Making things?") asked Nightfall just as anxiously. ("Making what sort of thing?")

Helplessly West Wind sent an image, a kind of wooden panel covered in hide. ("Do you know what it might be, First Ones?") she asked. ("We scouts don't like the look of it at all.")

("No,") said Avalanche, ("but I don't like the look of it either. I hope it isn't some kind of magic.")

("Er,") said Aristeas, and they all looked at him. ("It's a shield,") he told them.

They all shot a question-sense at him.

("A shield,") he repeated wretchedly. ("My people use them a lot. You hold one on your left arm, and it shelters you in battle. It—it might ward off rocks.")

There was a dreadful silence, and then Avalanche asked, ("How do they know about this shield thing?")

("I told Hyrgis,") he confessed miserably. ("I was singing a song about one, and he asked what it was about, and I told him. I—I told him in your language because that was easier than trying to translate into the northern speech, and—and he must have got some very useful images of it from me, enough to . . . let him make one. I'm sorry. I'm very sorry.")

There was another long silence. No one reproached him—not for giving Hyrgis the idea for a shield, not for sparing Hyrgis's life and so allowing him to warn Colaxis in time for the Arimaspians to escape the ambush. It made it worse, somehow; if they had reproached him, he could have argued and been angry, but now he just felt ashamed. Then he felt horribly angry with Apollo. Why had the god sent him here if all he could do was make things worse? If Apollo meant him to defeat the Arimaspians, why was he shielding them? What did Apollo want?

It was the fatal question, the one he'd refused to consider when Blizzard put it to him. As he asked it—angrily and in silence—the answer leaped out at him like a landscape revealed by a flash of lightning. His own kind, as Nightfall had just said, had been happy to kill griffins in the past. He found himself blinking stupidly as he understood what would happen if the griffins succeeded in crushing the Arimaspians.

("So,") said Avalanche at last, ("they can get through the ravine and have some protection against the rocks. And they still have bows. Excellent, Blizzard")—she sounded almost pleading—("can you do *anything* about those bows?")

Blizzard and Aristeas had been examining the captured

bows all afternoon, trying to understand the spells that made them work. ("I'm sorry,") Blizzard said now, wearily, ("we can't break the spells on the bows. The only way to do that is to destroy them completely, and you have to have hold of them to do that.")

There was a stillness, and then Avalanche rested her head against her wing and said, ("Well then, we must attack, and suffer the losses.")

("No!") said Aristeas. ("Enough of your people have died already, and all because I wouldn't listen to my master. Blizzard, you were right. I knew you were right before, but I pretended to myself that you were wrong because I wanted to finish the business quickly and easily and go home. But I do understand why the god sent me here now, and I'll do what's necessary.")

("What do you mean?") asked Avalanche. ("Blizzard, what does he mean?")

("A few days ago I told him that I thought the battle wouldn't settle things,") Blizzard said, even more wearily, ("and I told him that we should ask for help from the ones beyond the wind.")

("Oh, Blizzard!") said Avalanche in disgust. ("The last thing we need is to lose our excellent magician on a wild flight northward! We can't reach the place beyond the wind! I tried once when I was a youngster. I flew north till there was nothing but moss and reindeer and a wind like winter, but I never got beyond the wind.")

("You can't go beyond the wind by flying,") replied Blizzard evenly. ("But there is a way to get there. I learned it from my teacher Waterfall, who learned it from her teacher, who learned it from her teacher, who learned it from Gold-arrow of the beyond-the-wind ones.")

("Lightning-flash!") exclaimed Avalanche. ("Why didn't you use this before?")

("She should not use it at all,") interrupted Aristeas. ("It's a . . . very dangerous spell, and I don't think she's strong enough to do it and return. I can do it. I've done similar spells before.")

("No, Excellent!") said Blizzard urgently. ("I should do it. It's more complicated than I thought it was when I told you about it. I used magic yesterday to recall the details of the spell, and—and it will only work for a griffin.")

Aristeas winced. ("There isn't a human version?")

("I wouldn't know it if there was, would I?")

("So, in other words,") Aristeas said in horror, ("I'd have to reach the edge of death *twice* to perform this spell? Once to change my shape and once for the spell itself?")

("Yes.")

("Oh, by Apollo! Phoibos Apollo!") Aristeas sat still for a moment, thinking about it and feeling quite sick, then swallowed and shook himself. ("Well, if that's the case, I'd better do the shape changing at once. That will give me some time to recover before doing the travel spell tomorrow.")

("Excellent!") exclaimed Blizzard, shocked.

("Just be quiet!") he told her.

("What is this talk about dying?") demanded Avalanche in bewilderment.

("You say you've died before?") asked Nightfall skeptically.

("Not *died*,") Aristeas corrected briskly. ("Not all the way. But some spells can be worked only from the edge of death, and shape-changing spells are among them. I've done it once. I had to turn into a wolf—")

("Why?") asked Nightfall, even more skeptical.

("I'd been captured by the Neuroi,") Aristeas answered impatiently. ("They're a Scythian tribe; they all turn into wolves for a few days every year because of some curse. I entered their territory at the wrong season, and they took me prisoner and threatened to kill me. But when I told them I was a magician, they said that if I became a wolf with them, they'd spare me. So I turned into a wolf and went hunting with them. They were very kind to me afterward, declared me an honorary Neurian and their brother. Anyway, I know how shape changing's done, and I can do it now.")

The First Ones all stared, flabbergasted—except Blizzard, who just looked anxious. Firegold, on the other hand, seemed pleased.

("You're going to turn yourself into one of us tonight?") he asked delightedly. ("Wonderful! Can I fetch anything you need?")

("Herakles!") Aristeas exclaimed. ("This isn't a concert! I'll do it in my room, and I don't want anyone with me . . . except you, Blizzard, to help if anything goes wrong, and you, Firegold, to—to stand by me.")

Firegold was puzzled. ("Stand by . . . you sound as though you're afraid!")

("By Apollo, lord of Delos, killer of the Python! Of course, I am, you—you dandelion-brained piece of drift! I *hate* doing this!")

("Maybe you shouldn't,") said Blizzard.

("Of course he shouldn't!") said Avalanche. ("We need his help here, with the one-eyes.")

Aristeas set his teeth. ("I *can't* help here with the one-eyes. You know that as well as I do, Avalanche. Nobody can help. You fight them with things as they are, and win or lose, your people face death. As for you, Blizzard, don't go all doubtful on me now. I need your help.") Aristeas got to his feet. ("We'll need fire. Blizzard, put some pebbles in one of those gold dishes and then fill it with coals from the sacred fire. Firegold, you get another basin and fill it with clean drinking water. Both of you come along to my room now.")

The passage to his room was already dark, and he had to take the golden dish of coals from Blizzard to light his way. Most of the other caves were now occupied by the assembled griffins, who were settling down for the night. Aristeas set the bowl of coals on the east side of the cave he shared with Firegold, then took off his cloak and hung it across the doorway like a curtain. Firegold set down the basin of water, and Blizzard arranged it opposite the dish of fire. She looked at Aristeas anxiously. ("I've never done this,") she told him. ("I've never even seen it done.")

("Well, have you *heard* how it's done?") he asked her. ("Yes, but—")

("Fine. Then don't say anything. You probably won't need to do anything at all. Just don't let the fire go out.")

He took off his boots, then took off his tunic and spread it on the floor, the head end toward the east. He set his knife at the feet, then picked up his lyre and set it down against the north wall. His hands lingered a moment on the lovely curve of the frame, and he drew his fingers quickly across the strings, calling out a ripple of music. He thought of how those fingers would become clumsy claws and started shaking. "O Apollo!" he whispered out loud. ("Blizzard, I had a dream . . .") He stopped himself. ("Never mind. Blizzard, how will I be able to work the second spell if I can't play the lyre and can't sing?")

("But you sing with your mind,") she said. ("You've done that all along.")

He realized that she was right and bowed his head. He gave one more glance at his preparations and thought of something else. ("When I became a wolf,") he told the griffins, ("the Neuroi gave me a wolfskin. I don't think I need a skin, but I do need something to tell my body what shape it must take. Firegold, could you . . . well, lie down beside me at the appropriate time and put your wing over me? That should be enough.")

("Of course!") said Firegold. ("Just tell me when.")

Aristeas sighed. ("Blizzard will have to tell you when. I won't be able to. You must understand: I'm going to bring myself to the instant of death—and stop there. But death won't pause for long. When you act, you'll have to do it quickly. Well then, I'd better start.")

He turned toward the east and raised his arms, as the Greeks did in prayer, and began by singing a hymn to Apollo. He found that it steadied him, and when he picked up his knife and cut three locks of his own hair, his hands hardly shook at all. He dropped the hair onto the fire, still singing, and the coals began to glow more brightly, so that he could see his shadow and the shadows of the two griffins cast very dark against the rocky walls. He washed his hands three times in the water, then splashed it three times over his head. His own voice seemed to come from some other part of him now, as though the wall or the fire were singing, while he himself had moved into another room. He held his hands over the fire, singing the great invocation, then slowly reached down and picked up a single brilliant coal. It did not burn him, and as he continued to sing, it glowed brighter and brighter, until the whole room was lit with a radiance like the sun. Holding the light above his head, looking into it and singing, he lay down on his back upon the tunic. Slowly his hands came down and set the coal on his bare chest, just above the heart.

There was a moment of intense pain, and then he was standing and looking down at himself lying there, teeth clenched and neck arched in agony. Then the body slumped and was still, the eyes staring sightlessly upward. The white-hot coal on its chest began to cool.

("Now, Firegold!") cried Blizzard.

("But,") said Firegold, frightened and bewildered, ("but he's dead!")

("Not yet! Hurry! Before the fire cools!")

Shaking, Firegold dropped down beside the body with a ridiculous little cheep of distress and spread his wings. Aristeas, standing by the lyre, saw his own face vanish under Firegold's trembling golden pinions. He knelt down and pressed his left hand against the spread wing. The hand sank into the wing and through it, and beneath the feathers he could feel the misty shape of his own face. He drew his right hand from Firegold's head to his own and began singing, without sound and without words. He felt the mist begin to change, rapidly at first, then slowing, slowing painfully. The coal was cooling. He must hurry. If it died before the spell was completed, his own death would be final. He stood again and looked out eastward, and in this bodiless shape he could see through the stone of the Fortress to the moon rising beyond the mountains. He turned to it and sang the final part of the spell.

There was a jolt, and he felt something burning into his chest. He raised his hand to move it aside, but his hand didn't move as it should. There was a squawk beside him, and then Firegold jumped away, looking terrified and, in some hard-to-define way, *different.* Aristeas tried again to knock away the burning thing, then rolled to shake it loose. A dying coal skittered across the floor. Blizzard darted after it, knocked it to the center of the room, then quickly splashed water on it, putting it out. Aristeas got to his hands and knees, tried to stand, and fell over.

("Lie still!") urged Blizzard, hurrying over to him.

When she was directly in front of him, bits of her seemed to vanish, and he found he could keep her in view only by turning his head away from her. Something was in front of his face. He tried to brush it away with his hand—and saw a claw sweep up, felt it clatter against his beak. He gave a cry, which came out as a squawk from a throat become tight and strange.

("O gods!") he said, and closed his eyes. It occurred to him that he ached all over and felt sick.

("Lie still,") said Blizzard again. ("It's done.")

("Excellent?") asked Firegold wonderingly.

("O gods!") Aristeas repeated miserably. ("Now I can never go home.")

("Of course you can,") soothed Blizzard. ("These spells are easier to reverse than to cast, aren't they? And I saved the coal you used. That will help, won't it? You've changed shapes before and gone back to being human. You can do it this time, too.")

Aristeas tried to groan, but the sound came out so horrible, half squawk and half cheep, that he stopped at once. Instead he put his head against his wing, then realized that this was what the griffins did, and defiantly rested it on his claws instead. ("Put the coal somewhere safe,") he told Blizzard. ("Put—put it next to the lyre. Oh, I feel dreadful!")

Firegold thought for a moment. ("Maybe you'd like a hot bath?") he suggested.

It took Aristeas a few tries to get to his feet and a few more tries to work out the half-slink half-hop walk of the griffins. He was staggering groggily down the passageway toward the hot springs, with Blizzard supporting him on one side and Firegold on the other, when Nightfall came up.

("The other First Ones sent me to find out what's happening,") he said, then, noticing Aristeas, asked in surprise, ("Who's this and what happened to him?")

("It's Excellent,") said Blizzard.

("*Excellent!*") exclaimed Nightfall, so forcefully that a number of other griffins poked their heads out of their rooms to see what was happening.

("You don't need to stare at me like that,") Aristeas said sharply. ("I told you what I was going to do.")

Nightfall's feathers stood up like a thistle. ("Lightning-flash!") he exclaimed in awe. ("It *is* Excellent.")

("Oh, be quiet and go away!") said Aristeas.

But Nightfall followed, fascinated, as Aristeas staggered down the passage to the baths. ("Will you—will you come back to the meeting tonight?") he asked.

("No,") said Aristeas sourly. ("You think doing this was easy? Tonight I'm having a bath and going straight to sleep. Anyway, the meeting has nothing to talk about. Good night!")

In the morning all the aches were gone, and he felt better, though not very much happier. He remembered from his time as a wolf that the longer one stayed in a changed body, the more the body's instincts took over from the human ones. He found that already he could move easily, without having to think what to do with each foot and foreclaw, and he sat up and began to preen his new feathers. The night before he had lain down in the hot water like a human, instead of sitting and splashing it over fluffed-up feathers like a griffin, and his plumage had instantly felt like a soggy woolen blanket and was now badly in need of attention. He was combing it straight with his beak when Firegold woke up with a start and stared at him.

("Good morning,") said Aristeas pointedly.

Firegold sat up. ("Good morning . . . Excellent,") he

said hesitantly. After a moment he added, ("You look very well.")

Aristeas ruffled his crest and looked at Firegold sourly from one eye. Then he went back to preening his left wing.

("You're much younger than I thought you were,") said Firegold, after another minute.

("What?") asked Aristeas.

("I can't tell human ages. I suppose I thought you were old because the only other magician I knew was Blizzard, and she's old. But you're not very much older than I am, are you? It's so strange seeing you as one of our kind. I can tell all sorts of things that I couldn't before. Last night I was so frightened when you changed that I almost couldn't do what you'd asked me to.")

("I know. I *was* there.")

("Yes, but you were dead then.")

("You think I wasn't aware of what was happening because of that?") Aristeas shook out the wing awkwardly and nearly knocked himself off his feet with the force of its sweep. ("O gods!") he said miserably, looking at it. ("I hope I don't have to use this thing today.") He folded the wing and looked at his reflection in the gold mirror. He saw a small, fierce griffin with feathers of a very dark bronze color, a lot like Nightfall, and shook his head sadly.

("I'll see what I can fetch us for breakfast,") offered Firegold soothingly.

Breakfast was awkward. Aristeas found that the thought of cooked meat had become nauseating. But so was the thought of eating it raw. It was only when Firegold started tearing a freshly killed rabbit into strips in front of him that Aristeas discovered that he was hungry enough to stomach it, though he still had to swallow it quickly with his eyes closed. His body liked the taste well enough, though.

When the meal was over, he felt well enough to face
the thing he had to do next and walked up the passageway
to the assembly hall, twitching his tail, with Firegold trailing behind.

The First Ones were still meeting. For all he could tell,
they'd been meeting all night. Blizzard wasn't there, but
the other three were sitting on their boulders with droop-
ing feathers and haggard eyes, and their voices as Aristeas
came in had the irritable tone of people who've been trying
for hours to think of a new idea and have succeeded only
in turning over a lot of old ones. They all stopped, however, when they saw Aristeas.

("That's Excellent,") explained Nightfall, and they all
stared as Aristeas strode up to the fire well and stopped
beside it, lashing his tail.

("Good morning,") said Avalanche after a moment.
("You're much younger than we thought you were.")

("I don't know why everyone seems to have believed
that I was ancient,") Aristeas remarked acidly. ("Where's
Blizzard?")

("She isn't up yet,") said Driftfeather.

("Do you really mean to go beyond the wind?") asked
Nightfall.

("Of course I do. You think I'd have done this to myself for pleasure?")

("I don't know,") said Driftfeather. ("You're much
better-looking than you were.") She straightened one of
her neck feathers, and Aristeas realized for the first time
that she was about his own age and that she was extremely
beautiful. He was taken aback and ruffled his own feathers.

("It still seems to us that it's lunacy for you to go,")
said Nightfall. ("We've been talking over the situation, and
we've had a few ideas that we think would do some damage

to our enemies and reduce our own losses in a battle. But
we were all sure that you'd be able to think of more. And
if you used your magic—")

("I cannot use magic to kill. You know that. I can't
help you by staying here. I've told you, I know now why
Apollo sent me. There are two reasons, and one of them
is to do with your people. I understand now that you are
in even greater danger than I'd realized. You think you're
numerous and powerful, but I traveled for two years to
reach you, through human nations as numerous as flies
swarming over a river, and I can see that you are only the
remnants of a nation, one small tribe clinging to its last
stronghold in these mountains. Even if you succeed in defeating the one-eyes, you are facing extermination.
Weaken them badly, and you will find the Issedones moving in from the west and taking their lands. And the
Issedones believe you to be no more than animals—gold-
hoarding, cattle-killing animals. They would be more dangerous to you than the one-eyes are. You will die if you
destroy the one-eyes. And you will die if you don't.")

There was a shocked silence. Blizzard entered the hall
by one of the other passages and stopped, watching.

("Then why have you taken our shape?") asked Driftfeather at last. ("To die with us?")

("No!") returned Aristeas forcefully. ("Half of the task
the god sent me here for is to save you, and to find the
way to do that, I have to go beyond the wind.")

("Half the task is to save us?") asked Blizzard, coming
forward. ("What is the other half?")

("To save the one-eyes,") replied Aristeas.

Beyond the Wind

9

The First Ones stared at him as though they suspected shape changing had driven him insane. Aristeas paid no attention and turned to Blizzard. ("I'm glad you're up,") he told her. ("Can you explain this travel spell to me? I hope I don't have to fly for it.")

("But you do,") said Blizzard. ("That's the reason I said it couldn't be done by a human.")

He'd suspected as much, but he still gave a shriek of rage and lashed his tail, which felt very satisfying. ("Well, then,") he said, resignedly, ("I suppose I'd better learn to fly. I hope I have some instincts for it, at least.") He started for the passage that led to the entrance of the Fortress.

("But what do you mean, save the one-eyes?") Drift-feather called after him.

He turned back, reluctantly because now that he knew what he had to do, he wanted to get it over with as quickly as possible. The First Ones were still staring at him in stunned disbelief. He ruffled his feathers unhappily and began to explain the things he'd at last understood the night before. ("The one-eyes are all under a curse. I knew that

before, but I didn't understand what it meant. Their ancestress, a witch, sealed up their eyes so they couldn't weep.
It's made them so strong that they consider themselves no
longer human and see fit to despise the gods, but it's destroyed them. Since that spell was laid on them, they've
been unable to learn. The nations around them have made
new things—strengthened bows, woven cloth, and forged
metal—but the one-eyes still dress in skins and use axes
of stone like their ancestors, and even when they capture
a bow, they break it. I think they're imprisoned in their
own strength, and that's what makes them so cruel. The
curse must be broken; they must be made fully human
again. That's what Apollo's oracle means by 'sealed eyes
shall break in weeping springs.' But I don't know how to
do it, and I can only hope the people beyond the wind can
tell me.") He stopped. The First Ones still looked stunned
and bewildered. Aristeas ruffled his feathers again, then
gave up trying to explain, shook his wings, and said,
("Blizzard, can you come along and explain the travel spell
to me while I try to work out how to fly?")

Blizzard did not explain the spell while he tried to work
out how to fly. Working out how to fly needed far too
much attention for him to do it and learn magic at the
same time. When Aristeas looked down from the ledge before the Fortress entrance and saw the mountainside falling
sheer for a thousand feet to a slope of ice and black rock,
he almost turned tail and went back inside. ("What if I
can't fly?") he asked.

("You can,") said Firegold. ("Just hold on to the rock
with your foreclaws and practice beating your wings. No,
hold on!") Aristeas, who hadn't held on, had knocked himself flat by the force of his own lopsided wingbeats. Firegold helped him up. ("Try again,") Firegold urged. ("Beat

your wings. No, together. That's right . . . keep beating them. Now you can let go of the rock. Let go! That's right! See? You went straight back. Now, try again. This time let go and jump with your hind legs at the same time. Very good! You were airborne that time. Now, one more time. Jump! Keep beating your wings, that's right! You've done it!")

Aristeas found himself flapping frantically upward from the ledge, straining every muscle and afraid to look down. Firegold leaped upward and followed him. ("You don't have to keep flapping your wings now,") he called.

Aristeas looked down at Firegold, saw the distance he had to fall, and beat his wings even more frantically. ("I'll fall!") he shouted.

("No, you won't. Hold still and you'll glide . . . not that way!") as Aristeas glided straight at a cliff. ("No!") as he began flapping again and moved toward it even faster. ("Swing your *tail* left, *left*, not right! There! Now a few more flaps . . . I think you're mastering it.")

Aristeas hung suspended between the cliff and the mountainside, holding on to the air with his pinions. Below him the slopes fell away. The wind that had boomed and chilled when he was human now lifted and supported him, and as his terror faded, he found that he could move in the wind by a twitch of a wing or curve of a tail. He circled upward with Firegold just behind him and watched the fields of rock give way to snow that glittered in the light of the morning sun. Then the air beneath him seemed to shudder, and he grabbed the wind with his feathers instinctively.

("What was that?") he asked Firegold.

("Air turbulence,") explained Firegold. ("It is a little unsteady this morning. Perhaps there'll be a storm later.")

("There will be,") said Blizzard, and Aristeas twisted his head about and saw her drifting upward behind them.

("Is that weather sense or something to do with the spell?") he asked.

("Well, both,") said Blizzard, coming beside him with a few flaps of her wings. ("I think there'd be a storm anyway, but there will certainly be a storm if you work the travel spell.")

("Why should a travel spell affect the weather?") Aristeas asked suspiciously. ("I've never done a spell that affected the weather. It's not forbidden to me, but I've never done it.")

("The spell uses the lightning to draw you beyond the wind.")

Aristeas grabbed at the air again, though there hadn't been any turbulence. ("I have to let myself be hit by lightning?") he cried.

("Blizzard!") exclaimed Firegold in horror. ("You can't mean that!")

Blizzard flinched. ("But I'm afraid it's true; that's the spell. If Excellent performs it correctly, in one flash of the lightning he will be where he wishes.")

Aristeas turned and soared in the opposite direction for a moment. The movement stopped him from thinking, and the feeling of the wind over his feathers was calming. ("Very well,") he said at last. ("After all I've done to be able to work this spell already, I can't possibly back out now. Blizzard, explain it to me. Firegold, why don't you go make some arrangements for a funeral? I might as well have some company on the wings of the lightning.")

("No, Excellent!") protested Firegold, very distressed. ("You can't. Not take the lightning's path while you're still alive. Last night was dreadful enough; you can't possibly do this horrible thing today!")

("When else am I supposed to do it? Today or, more likely, tonight, when they have some cover from the darkness, the one-eyes will be marching back up that ravine and on toward the Shoulder of the World. I have to get beyond the wind and back before they reach it. Oh, but, Firegold, when you've told the others there's going to be a funeral, do come back up here. I don't know how to get down, and you're good at explaining.")

Firegold told the other griffins that there would be a funeral and returned to instruct Aristeas on how to land, as he managed to do on the fifth attempt and with a bit of a bump. By then the bodies were being carried down from the snows and prepared for Sky-fire Mountain: the thirty-nine griffins who had died in the battle with the Arimaspians; Sunstrike, who'd guarded Hyrgis and been killed by him; and the mangled form of Wing-shadow, still on the battered stretcher, and looking even more pitiful than it had before. The griffins washed all the bodies with clean water and sprinkled them with gold dust—the ashes of the sacred earth-fire, they said, would bless them on their way to the sky. Then the friends and family of the dead eased them onto slings, and carried them out, up above the Shoulder of the World. Driftfeather, who had a relative among the dead, took charge of the funeral party. Avalanche and Nightfall remained at the Fortress to plan the defense against the Arimaspians, who were still building shields. The sky was clouding over, and the air had grown even more turbulent.

("Lightning-flash is coming to help you,") Blizzard told Aristeas as they flew behind the funeral party.

("If Lightning-flash really is the same as Apollo, he's helped me into unpleasant things for most of my life,") returned Aristeas. ("I wish he'd help someone else.")

("You'll feel differently when all this is done with, and you remember it, sitting among the white stone trees of your home.")

("Home!") said Aristeas longingly. ("Yes, I'd suffer almost anything to get home.")

Sky-fire Mountain was at the end of the great ridge that formed the Shoulder of the World, about an hour's flight from the Fortress. The high peaks dropped down into the valley, but just where they ended there was one last spur, jutting out against the blue distance. The top of this peak was slightly flat, still covered with the winter snow. The gold-dusted bodies were laid upon it, and then the family and friends flew around it in wide circles, going against the sun, singing long images of blackness and grief. The sky continued to darken, and there was an ominous rumble of thunder.

("We'd better take shelter now,") said Driftfeather. ("There's a cave in the next peak there, Excellent, where people usually watch to be sure that all goes well.")

("You'd better go there then,") said Aristeas.

("*We'd* better? What are you going to do?")

("Didn't Firegold tell you?")

("No,") said Firegold himself, soaring up from his place not far behind Aristeas. ("I didn't say, because I don't think you should do it, Excellent.")

("What does he mean to do now?") asked Driftfeather as though she dreaded the answer.

("Blizzard's spell to go beyond the wind is the path of the lightning,") replied Firegold before Aristeas could speak.

Driftfeather was horrified. She tried to order Aristeas not to work the spell, then, when he impatiently refused to listen to her, turned on Blizzard and furiously reproached the old magician for ever suggesting the idea. Firegold joined in, and then the rest of the funeral party. Aristeas lost his temper.

("By all the gods and heroes!") he shouted at them, so forcefully they all flinched. ("Do you think I *like* the idea of being hit by lightning? You think it's something we Greeks do for pleasure, that whenever we have a particularly fine festival, we run out in the rain and delight in burning ourselves to cinders? Herakles! I've told you why I have to do this, and if you had griffin brains in those narrow little skulls of yours, instead of the brains of geese, you'd understand and try to be *helpful* about it instead of making me and Blizzard miserable. By Apollo! Here I am, one wretched god-ridden Ionian enchanter, facing death for the second time in two days, and all you can do is cause difficulties, 'No, Excellent, you can't do that, Excellent!' Just be quiet and get into shelter! I'm summoning the storm!")

Most of the funeral party fled. Firegold remained for a moment, wailing ("But, Excellent!") until Aristeas brutally shouted at him to go. Then there was only Blizzard, soaring silently behind him.

Aristeas turned and began to circle sunwise. The air was very turbulent now. It shivered and kicked beneath his wings, and from the east the clouds swept up towering and black. ("You, too, Blizzard,") ordered Aristeas.

("Excellent,") she said miserably, ("I should be doing this, not you. . . . If I'm wrong, if I've forgotten some detail of the spell, if you . . .")

("Go away!") Aristeas told her. ("Now! And don't listen to what the others say. You're right, and they're wrong.")

Blizzard turned and dropped away, then flapped along

the ridge after the others, a small white figure flying against the dark rocks. Aristeas lowered his tail and swept upward, and the wind kicked and tore at him. He drove every thought from his mind and began to sing—not a human song, this time, but a griffin one of images flickered and held. Spiraling around and around the flattened top of Sky-fire Mountain, he sang the spell Blizzard had taught him, and the storm swept down upon him.

The first crack of lightning exploded eastward, and the thunder followed it. The wind was now so fierce, and the turbulence so great, that he could no longer guide himself; he simply clung to the air with every feather, and it screamed as it whirled him around and around the mountain. The rain came with a crash, and his feathers at once were drenched; he shivered, but couldn't feel the cold for the images singing in his skull. Then the lightning struck, and everything was made of fire. For one endless instant he flew burning in the middle of a great flock of griffins, and one of them, looking back over her shoulder, seemed to be Wing-shadow, and then he was falling. Down, down, and down; he thought of the rocks and tried to beat his wings but couldn't move. Down and down; he seemed to be falling forever. And then he realized that he wasn't falling but rising—floating upward through bubbling green water shot with rainbows. Again he struggled, and this time his wings stirred the water, and his legs kicked feebly, and suddenly his head burst into air. He kicked out, felt land beneath his feet, and crawled up to collapse gasping upon the edge of a deep green pool.

For a long time he lay still, aware of nothing except the pounding of his own heart and the rasping of breath in his lungs. Then, gradually, he began to notice things around him. He was lying on thick, soft moss, and the sun was hot on his back. Birds were singing, and there was a scent of flowers—jasmine, he thought, and wild thyme. He lifted his head and saw trees above him, tall trees of a kind he'd never seen before, with long, feathery leaves, studded with white and gold flowers. He pulled his forelegs under himself and looked around. Behind him a waterfall tumbled over a rocky ledge and plunged, foaming, into the pool, covering itself in rainbows. A brightly colored bird flitted among the trees, pecking at clusters of orange fruit. The largest butterfly he'd ever seen fanned brilliant green wings by the edge of the water as it drank.

Aristeas hauled himself onto his hindquarters and sat up. His feathers were drenched, too heavy with water to let him fly. His muscles all felt weak and trembled with shock, but he shook himself, beat his wings, then tried to squeeze the moisture from his sodden feathers with his beak. Then he heard voices—human voices, singing. He took a step toward them, then stopped. What would humans make of him in this shape? They were as likely to kill him as help him.

He was still wondering whether and where to hide when the owners of the voices appeared under the trees opposite him. They were two fair-haired boys, dressed in brightly colored kilts, and to Aristeas's relief, the most dangerous weapon they carried was a bucket. They saw Aristeas and stopped both their singing and their movement forward. There was a moment of total silence; even the waterfall's noise seemed deadened. Then the taller of the boys dropped his bucket with a thump and shrieked, "Look!" He screamed it in the northern language that the Issedones and Arimaspians used.

Aristeas spread his wings nervously, wondering if he'd be able to fly while he was so wet. But the boys didn't seem afraid of him; they both were beaming at him. "It's a griffin!" cried the younger boy, shrieking with excitement. "Look, a griffin's come! And we found him!" Then, to Aristeas's surprise, he spread his arms out and said, very loudly and very slowly, "Welcome, friend!"

The taller boy shoved him impatiently. "He can't understand you," he said. "Look, you're frightening him with that shouting. Griffins talk with pictures behind the eyes, and sounds don't mean anything to them."

"Hellooo, griffin," the smaller boy said, more quietly this time, with the same big gesture of the arms.

"He won't understand!" repeated the taller boy. "We need to fetch Abaris; he knows griffin-talk."

Aristeas shook his wings and flicked his tail in amazement. "Hello," he said cautiously. He said it with his mind, but in the northern language, not in flicker-talk. "I do understand. Can you hear me?"

The boys both jumped, jaws dropping, and then the smaller one beamed again. "You can talk our language perfectly well, by magic!" he exclaimed happily, and gave his fellow a told-you-so look. "Yes, we can hear you. Hello! Welcome!"

The taller boy looked confused. "But Abaris said . . . oh, I understand now! Please excuse me, sir. You must be a griffin magician, who's learned our language."

"I am a magician," Aristeas said, now thoroughly bewildered. "I was trying to reach the place beyond the wind."

"Then you've reached it," said the taller boy. He pulled himself up, took a deep breath, and declared, self-consciously, "And you are very welcome here, sir! In the name of the old friendship between our peoples, welcome! Can we bring you to talk to Abaris?"

Aristeas turned his head sideways to stare at them. He wasn't sure what he'd expected beyond the wind, but this excited welcome certainly wasn't it, and he didn't know what to make of it. And he'd heard stories about a Hyperborean magician called Abaris. But those stories were hundreds of years old. Perhaps Abaris was a kind of title and meant something like "king" or "governor." "I've come to ask help with a question of magic," he told the boys.

"Then you do want to talk to Abaris," the taller boy said eagerly. "Can we show you the way, sir?"

Wonderingly Aristeas nodded. He walked unsteadily around the edge of the pool, and the two boys excitedly waved him onto a path that he now saw went through the trees.

The path led to a town of brightly painted houses. There were plenty of people around, and when they saw Aristeas, they each stopped short, then came running, shouting, and exclaiming excitedly that a griffin had crossed the boundary to visit them. A beautiful girl ran forward and draped a chain of flowers over his shoulders. The two boys strutted more proudly with each step. By the time they reached the temple they were followed by a large crowd.

Aristeas recognized the building as a temple at once, though it didn't look like the Greek temples he was used to, except for the columns of the porch around it. It was round, and its dome had been gilded so that it glowed as warm and bright as the griffins' assembly hall, and it was much the biggest building in the town. The crowd stopped outside it, and some men and women in white hurried out to see what they wanted.

"This is a griffin magician who's come to see Abaris!" said the taller boy. "We found him at the sacred pool."

"In the name of the old friendship, be welcome!" cried the men and women in white, beaming at Aristeas. "It has been many, many years since anyone has crossed the boundary from the Shoulder of the World."

They held open the door of the temple, and after a moment's hesitation Aristeas walked in. The men and women in white followed him, along with the two boys and the whole crowd of townspeople laughing and talking.

The inside of the temple was shadowy after the sunshine outside. It smelled of incense, and the walls glowed with paintings and with gold. Aristeas was led through the great circular hall, into a passageway at the back, and out another door into a small courtyard where a man sat on a bench under a grapevine, playing upon a lyre.

"Abaris!" called the two boys, pushing past everyone else and bursting in both together. "Look, we found a griffin at the sacred pool! He's come here to talk to you."

The man set down the lyre and stood up. He was tall and, like most of the Hyperboreans, fair-haired and blue-eyed. And the moment Aristeas saw him, he knew he was looking at a very great magician.

Abaris bowed his head. ("Welcome, fellow magician!") he said, in flicker-talk. ("It's been a long time since we had a visit from one of the children of gold. What brings you from the Shoulder of the World?")

Now that he had reached his goal, Aristeas didn't know what to say. He ruffled his wet feathers and twitched his tail.

"You don't have to talk to him in pictures," said the tall boy. "He understands human speech."

Abaris looked surprised. "Do you?" he asked out loud. He had a deep, musical voice. "You must have spent some time in human form then."

"All my life," replied Aristeas. "I only took this shape last night, so that I could reach you by the path of the lightning."

Abaris looked even more surprised. "The path of the lightning is, as I well remember, a hard one, and shape changing is even worse. Who are you, and why did you need to reach me so badly that you were willing to face death twice to do it?"

"I am a Greek from the city of Proconnesus. My name is Aristeas. I have been sent by Apollo to break the curse on the Arimaspians and to give safety to the griffins."

Abaris whistled. "Apollo has not given you an easy task, then, Aristeas of Proconnesus. But we are all servants of the god here, and we will help you in any way we can."

Aristeas felt much happier after this. The men and women in white shooed the crowd away with instructions to "let the magicians talk!" The two boys protested loudly that the griffin was their guest but had to go as well, and Aristeas sat down in the warm sunshine of the courtyard and began talking.

He told Abaris everything that had happened: how he'd left Proconnesus; how he'd tried to go back and hadn't been able to; how Hyrgis and Skylas had captured him and how he'd learned their plans and gone to the Fortress with Firegold; how he'd seen Colaxis and the prophecy from the Delphic oracle.

"I know something about that!" exclaimed Abaris. "There was an Arimaspian woman, a very powerful witch, who reached the boundary of this land about ten years ago. I met her there and talked to her. She said she wanted to consult the god about the future. I thought that was just an excuse and that really she had some plan to increase her power by stealing magical things from us, and I told her that her kind was forbidden to enter our land, and she should send to Delphi. I told her how to do that and gave her a spell of interpretation to use on the reply. But it seems she really did send to Delphi, and the god answered her! Answered her with an oracle, and with you as well! So, the Arimaspians have been accursed long enough, and their humanity will be restored. Wonderful news!"

"You sound as though you've been wanting to break the curse for years!" exclaimed Aristeas, taken aback.

"Nobody who's seen them would want to keep them as they are," replied Abaris. "I spent years trying to think of a way to break the curse, but by the time I'd thought of it, it was too late for me to do it. That needs someone in the human world, someone like you."

"But—but I don't know how to break the curse!" Aristeas protested. "That was one of the things I came here to find out!"

"*One* of the things?" asked Abaris. "What other reasons did you have?"

"As I said before, I have to learn how to save the griffins. I can see perfectly well that they aren't safe even if I succeed in breaking the curse. Making the Arimaspians human again would only stop their immediate attack; it wouldn't make them friendly in the future. I need something more, but I've no idea what."

"Don't you?" Abaris's face had taken on a suspicious look.

"Very well," admitted Aristeas, turning his head sideways to return the look. "I did have an idea, but I don't know how it can be done. I would like the griffins to come here, beyond the wind."

"I was afraid that you were thinking of that," said Abaris. "What makes you think we want them here?"

Aristeas glared at him. "You've said you're servants of Apollo."

"And so we are. But are the griffins?"

"They worship the gods!"

"They worship griffin gods, Lightning-flash and Earth-fire. Do you know what they look like? They have wings and tails."

Aristeas lashed his own tail. "So?"

"Do you think Apollo has a tail?"

"Apollo is a god, not a man!" Aristeas snapped. "If you really are the Abaris of the stories, the Abaris I've heard about, who traveled all over the world, you know perfectly well that gods have many forms. Even in the stories gods often take the forms of things that aren't human. Apollo has appeared as a wolf; Zeus as a swan and a bull and a shower of gold. The griffins honor their gods. They were even willing to accept me, a human like those who have done them great injury in the past, because the god had sent me. When they have such respect for Apollo, it's disgraceful for you to talk about Lightning-flash like that!"

Abaris laughed. "Well done!" he exclaimed. "I'm sorry, Aristeas. I said that to test you. I had to know your real feelings toward the griffins because if you want to help them, it will be hard. In fact, as perhaps you noticed, my own people have the friendliest of feelings toward the griffins, and I can promise you that they would agree to do almost anything to shelter them from destruction. But the thing you want will be very difficult to achieve. You know yourself that the path of the lightning is one that very few can travel and live."

"But there must be another way. You said that you met Colaxis at the boundary. At what boundary, where?"

Abaris sighed. "Let me explain to you what this land

is. It used to be a full part of the human world, a place you could ride to, if you went beyond the land of the Issedones. But we were a more settled people than our neighbors, growing crops and cultivating all the arts—but especially the art of magic. Our neighbors were warlike and always threatening to rob us and steal our lands and goods. We hated war and killing, so we defended ourselves by magic, enchanting our boundaries and making it hard for our enemies to find us. Then the climate was harsh, and the winters cold, harming our crops, so we cast spells to make it milder. We piled enchantment on enchantment over many years, and it began to change us. Magic has grown common among us, so that most of us have at least a touch of it. But we've drifted farther and farther from the world, and it's grown harder and harder for us to cross the boundaries of our own land, so that now only a great magician can do so, and then only at great cost. Yes, Colaxis found the boundary. But she couldn't cross it. Nor can I, though I did once. I am hundreds of years old. Here my magic keeps me young, but if I set foot over the boundary, I would instantly turn to dust.

"I said that our people would welcome the griffins. They were our nearest neighbors, in the past, and the only ones who were also our friends. But the only way you could bring the whole tribe beyond the wind would be to extend our boundary so that it included the Shoulder of the World."

"Could that be done?" asked Aristeas.

Abaris looked very solemn. "Yes," he said quietly. "But it would not be easy. It would need at least three magicians in your world as well as all the strength we have here. And those three magicians would have to work the magic in complete freedom from self-will, having all of them renounced forever their heart's desire."

Aristeas found his feathers all standing on end. *"Three magicians.* Even if I were one—"

"You'd have to be," said Abaris.

"But even if I were, what good would it do? Say I'm one; say Blizzard is another. We're still one magician short—and even if I had time to travel and find another magician willing to help me, where would I find a human willing to renounce his heart's desire for the sake of the griffins?"

"I can't say," replied Abaris calmly. "But Apollo found one—didn't he? And if, as you believe, the god wants this to happen, you or he will find another. Once you've broken the curse on the Arimaspians, you should have time to search. But you must be willing to renounce your own heart's desire whatever comes. The spell to break the curse has the same requirement."

Aristeas gave a long griffin scream. He leaped to his feet and stood shaking with half-spread wings. He felt somehow that he'd known all along that this would happen, but now that it had, he felt he would have preferred even death in the lightning.

"You know what it is you must renounce," Abaris observed quietly.

"Yes," he answered savagely. "What did I ever do to Apollo, for him to treat me so cruelly? To accomplish what he wants, and to save my friends, I would have to accept that I can never go home."

Face-to-Face
10

Abaris explained how the two spells could be worked and promised to watch events in the outside world by his own magic and to prepare his own people's enchantments when Aristeas found a third magician to help him move the boundary. Then he asked if his visitor had had anything to eat or drink since arriving beyond the wind.

"No," said Aristeas. And he realized how hungry and thirsty he was. The absolute crimson fury he'd been feeling toward Apollo had stopped him from noticing before.

"Good!" said Abaris. "I thought everyone would know not to offer you anything, but someone could have forgotten. If you'd had anything, even a drink of water, you would have had to die again to leave this country. But as it is, you'll be able to fly out with just a simple spell to ease your passage."

Aristeas jerked his tail back and forth angrily. He was relieved that he could get back without facing death a third time, but relief didn't make him any less thirsty. It was a hot day beyond the wind. "I did preen some water off my feathers," he said. "I may have swallowed some."

"That was at the sacred pool? It will be all right then;

a very small amount of water from that pool won't have affected you. But you can't have anything else. If you're very thirsty, I'll escort you to the boundary now and help you lower it." Abaris picked up his lyre, slung it over his shoulder, and showed Aristeas back through the temple and out into the town. The eager crowd had to be shooed away again before the two could walk out into the countryside.

"You say most of those people have some magical powers?" Aristeas asked.

Abaris nodded. "Even the boys who greeted you are magicians of sorts," he said. "They wouldn't have been able to hear you otherwise."

"Then, since magic is so common here, why can't one of your people cross the boundary and do these spells?" Aristeas demanded resentfully. "I can see that *you* can't, if you'd turn to dust, but surely there are others who—"

Abaris shook his head. "The spell that sealed the eyes of the Arimaspians has been strong enough to hold a whole tribe under its curse for several centuries, and it needs a very great magician to break it. I might have done it when I was still in the human world, but at the time I didn't know how." He thought for a minute and added, "I suppose Opis might be able to do it, but she's far away in the Tin Isles, accomplishing some other task, and isn't likely to be back for years. I can't think of anyone else powerful enough."

"But if it's so difficult, why do you think I can do it?"

At this Abaris stared in surprise. "By Apollo!" he exclaimed. "Don't you realize what you are? Have you ever met a magician as powerful as you are—not counting me?"

Aristeas thought of all the magicians he'd ever met: the Greeks who sold good-luck charms in the marketplace and curses for enemies under the counter; the Scythian fortune-tellers with their bundles of magic sticks; the Bald People smiths with their secret whispers; the Neuroi with their wolfskins and spitting oaths. "Well, no," he admitted, surprised. "But—"

Abaris laughed. "You must be younger and a lot less experienced than I thought. I never can tell the age of a griffin. You are quite possibly the most powerful magician in the human world. That is why Apollo imposed this task on you—that, and the fact that you were willing to do it."

"But I'm *not* willing!" Aristeas protested. "If I could leave it and go home, I would."

Abaris smiled. "Why didn't you?"

"I told you. I was so tormented with anxiety over the mysterious disaster in the east that I couldn't rest."

"If you were really unwilling," said Abaris, "you would have rested. You would have woken when the god stirred you, and thought, 'Poor things, whoever they are, but there's nothing I can do, and maybe it's not real anyway,' and gone back to sleep. And after a while you wouldn't even have woken. And even now, if you were really unwilling, you would not be stiff with rage against the god; you'd have said at once, 'This sacrifice is obviously something someone else will do,' and you'd be going back quite peacefully."

"Wasn't I just asking you if someone else could do it?"

"No. You were asking me why someone else couldn't. You'd already assumed that you would. Here we are at the boundary."

No one looking at the boundary would have realized that it was there. Where Abaris and Aristeas had stopped, the path led through a field of tall grass, so high that it came above the knees of the horses grazing in it. Beyond, the field went on, though the grass became gradually shorter and scruffier, and hazy in the distance were the shapes of mountains. But Aristeas could feel the magic in the air like a curtain. He ruffled his feathers and wondered whether to walk out or to fly. His forelegs, which weren't really designed for walking, were already aching. On the other hand, the air was calm, and he was hot and thirsty, and it seemed too much effort to take off.

"Before you go back," said Abaris, "let me explain what you should do if you ever want to cross in human form. And let me say that I'd be delighted to welcome you back at any time, in any form, that you wish."

Aristeas thanked him, and a few minutes later the Hyperborean magician was playing on the lyre to ease his passage and Aristeas was walking across the boundary.

In three steps it began to get colder. In five steps the mountains stopped being hazy and distant and loomed above him. In seven steps Abaris had vanished, together with the field he stood in. The sound of the lyre continued for a moment, coming from thin air, and then stopped. Aristeas was alone on a rocky slope in the afternoon sunshine, with a strong, cold wind ruffling his feathers.

("Nothing to eat or drink here either,") he remarked to himself sourly. He spread his wings and was about to flap his way upward when a flicker-whisper of ("Excellent!") rustled behind his eyes. It seemed to echo in his mind afterward, like the waves from a stone dropped in a pool, one ripple after another flickering ("Excellent, Excellent, Excellent,") more and more faintly.

He paused. ("Yes?") he asked eagerly. The call seemed to him to be magic, and he guessed that Blizzard was trying to find him. ("I'm here.")

There was stillness. The slope lay bare and plain, patched with snow, and the wind hissed across his feathers.

("I'm here!") Aristeas repeated, more forcefully.

There was a sudden pounding in his mind, and then Colaxis was standing in front of him.

Aristeas shot backward into the air faster than he would have believed possible. He caught an outcropping of rock and perched there unsteadily, staring fearfully at the Arimaspian queen. She was standing in a patch of snow, but her feet hadn't sunk into it, and though the afternoon sun was bright, she cast no shadow. He realized with relief that this was only a spell she'd made to find him, and she wasn't really present at all. Now that he knew to look, he could make out, very dim and ghostly, the shape of her tent, where she really stood, and, also ghostlike, but growing clearer even as he watched, Hyrgis's form standing beside the queen's. The former scout was now wearing the white cloak of the queen's guards.

"Greetings—Excellent!" said Colaxis, pronouncing the name triumphantly. Of course, Aristeas thought, she needed to know my name to find me. Hyrgis could only tell her the griffin version of it, but it was enough, once I was away from all the clouding spells we put on the Fortress. "Do I see you in your true form now?" the queen went on.

"No," Aristeas replied. He said it the way he'd talked to Abaris, in the northern language spoken in the mind. He sat down on the outcrop of rock and turned his head to study Colaxis coolly. He'd been terrified when she appeared, but now he felt much more confident. She couldn't physically harm him when she wasn't physically here, and he was certain that he couldn't be ensorcelled by anyone if he didn't want to be. After all, he told himself smugly, I'm probably the most powerful magician in the world. "No, you can't escape the prophecy that way," he said. "Really

I'm an Ionian Greek from Proconnesus, and I only took this shape last night. The correct form of my name, incidentally, is Aristeas. Your . . . *associate* . . . there, who seems to have been promoted, should have checked the details."

This seemed to annoy Colaxis. "The only good thing that's come out of your presence here," she snarled, "is that I've realized how loyal and resourceful my servant Hyrgis really is." Hyrgis smirked. "Yes, I've made him the captain of my guard, and perhaps you know how he's been using the authority I've given him. He's taken an idea from your mind and turned it against you. Tonight our people will march through that ravine where you prepared an ambush, safe beneath our shields. Then we'll climb the rocks by a path my servant Hyrgis found and destroy the Fortress of the griffins!"

"I don't think so," replied Aristeas. "What do you want with me, queen of the Arimaspians?"

Colaxis smiled, though her eye was smoldering with hatred. "I have a proposal for you," she said. "If you're wise enough to accept it, we'll both benefit."

"Is this the proposal Hyrgis was trying to make before?" Aristeas asked, casually scratching his neck with one claw. "You give me a potion, and I go home? Because I wouldn't give any potion you'd brewed to a sick goat, let alone drink it myself."

Colaxis shook her head. "You've been beyond the wind, haven't you?" she whispered. "They know powerful magic there. I think you went to find a spell to destroy me, and most likely, they gave it to you. No, I can see I'll have to offer you something more substantial than a drug against the pangs of conscience. If you go home, I will withdraw all my forces from the mountains and make a treaty of peace with the griffins. To be rid of you, I am willing to let them live.''

Aristeas felt something like a jolt in the pit of his stomach and spread his wings with a little cry. He wasn't sure whether what shook him was hope or fear. "You—you wouldn't keep the treaty," he said uncertainly.

"I will bind myself to it with the strongest oaths and magic I know," said Colaxis.

"What about the Issedones?" Aristeas demanded.

"You may warn them that I intend to attack," replied Colaxis. "They can take their chances in a battle, surely? They're at war with their human neighbors anyway; why should you defend them against us but not against other humans?"

Aristeas stared at her in agony. If Colaxis left the griffins alone, they'd be safe—but only for a time. Her successors, or possibly the Issedones, would eventually move on the Shoulder of the World, tempted by the gold.

Yes, he thought, but then saving them would be someone else's problem—some Hyperborean magician or another foreigner chosen by Apollo. After all, if the god can send one Ionian, he could send another in twenty years or so. I wouldn't be leaving the griffins to certain death if I went home.

"I don't know," he said after a long silence. And he thought of Proconnesus. In memory the city was so lovely that he wanted to cry.

Colaxis's eye glowed. "Come," she said sweetly, "I know magic as well as you. Death-dealing spells are costly things. If you work the enchantment they taught you behind the wind, there will be a price to pay—your soul or your eyes or whatever you hold dearest. Isn't it better to achieve your goal without such a sacrifice?"

("Quiet!") Aristeas shouted. He didn't realized he'd used flicker-talk until Hyrgis winced.

"Oh, speaking like a griffin now, are you?" asked Colaxis. "You astonish me, magician. You say you're an Ionian Greek, but how much is that true anymore? Look at yourself! Wouldn't you do better to go back to your own people quickly, while you're still at least partly human?"

Aristeas fluffed up his feathers with rage. "I have nothing to say to you!" he shouted.

"But you'll think about my proposal," said Colaxis.

"I'll—I'll tell you my answer in the morning!" He leaped from the rock and flapped clumsily upward. Colaxis, smiling, vanished.

Shaking with anger, Aristeas glided about in circles, looking for the way back to the Fortress. In fact, it wasn't hard to find. He recognized the flat-topped spur of Sky-fire Mountain almost at once and realized that he'd been half-way into the valley he'd seen from the mountaintop.

There were no other griffins about. Someone, he told himself, should have waited. Someone should have been there, looking for him, hoping he was all right. Gods! Why should he give up everything for people who couldn't even be bothered to wait for him one day? Heavily he began to fly back along the Shoulder of the World.

By the time he reached the Fortress it was evening. He was very hungry, very exhausted, and he wallowed unreservedly in his misery, busily resenting the griffins' neglect, pitying himself, and raging against the god. He glided down to the entrance of the Fortress in the last of the afternoon sun and ignored the squawks of amazement from the griffin guarding it. He marched down the entrance passage into the assembly hall and found Drift-feather, Nightfall, and Avalanche sitting on their boulders, with Firegold beside them, wearily discussing the war in front of most of the assembled tribe. When he himself entered the hall, the discussion stopped abruptly in an absolute stunned silence. The whole golden hall stared.

("Don't greet me, then,") he said bitterly.

("Excellent!") shouted Firegold, and hurled himself across the hall. He pressed himself against Aristeas's wings like a cat, nearly knocking him over, leaned forward, and tenderly straightened some of Aristeas's neck feathers. ("Excellent! Oh, Lightning-flash! I thought I'd never see you again!")

("!") said Aristeas sourly. ("You could have waited for me to get back.")

The other griffins were now crowding around, exclaiming. The First Ones bounded over, crests going up and down with joy, and brushed the tips of Aristeas's wings or touched his claws with their beaks. ("We thought you were dead!") protested Firegold. ("We saw the lightning strike you. You're back, you're alive! Oh, sun-brightness, swiftness, sweet-water! Did you go beyond the wind?")

("Yes,") admitted Aristeas, softened by the passionate welcome.

("!!! What was it like?") asked Firegold eagerly.

("Hot,") replied Aristeas. ("Very hot. And I wasn't allowed to drink anything because it would make it harder to go back if I did. I'm perishing of thirst. But I met another magician there who taught me what I needed to know—and—and—") The meeting with Colaxis was tormenting him, and he suddenly saw a way to escape any painful decision about it. ("And when I got back, I met the witch-queen, and she made a peace proposal, which I'll tell you about. Where's Blizzard?")

It appeared that Blizzard was in her room, grieving for

Aristeas and reproaching herself for his death. Someone was sent to fetch her. Aristeas had a long drink of water.

Blizzard rushed into the hall before Aristeas had finished drinking and dropped onto her belly in front of him. ("Excellent!") she cried. ("I'm so sorry!")

("Whatever for?") he asked, taken aback.

("For sending you on the path of the lightning, which I was afraid to travel myself.")

("But your spell worked perfectly,") he said. ("Crash, bang, I was there—oh, but, Firegold, I think I saw Wing-shadow flying, in the instant the lightning hit me. She was flying off, with the others. She looked back. Anyhow, I went beyond the wind, and apart from being hot, it's a lovely place. I met a magician called Abaris. Remembering the stories I've heard of him, I *think* he's the same as your Gold-arrow. This is what he told me.")

He explained to the First Ones, and to the whole assembly, everything that Abaris had told him and, afterward, everything Colaxis had said.

("It doesn't surprise me that Gold-arrow said you were the greatest magician of the age,") said Blizzard when he'd finished.

("Excellent, your name fits you in every way,") declared Avalanche.

("Never have the griffins owed so great a debt to a member of another race as we owe to you,") said Nightfall solemnly.

("Stay with us and become a First One, please!") said Driftfeather.

Aristeas preened himself. He felt infinitely better. ("Yes, but,") he said, ("what do we say to the peace proposal?")

There was a silence, and then Avalanche said, ("I say, we accept it.")

The others nodded, except Driftfeather, who asked sadly, ("*Must* Excellent go then?")

("Driftfeather,") said Avalanche severely, ("he's human.")

("He's human, and he wants to be with his own people,") said Blizzard. ("I saw that in his heart when he first came here. We could never permit him to renounce his home for our sake.")

The others, even Driftfeather, agreed. Aristeas sat looking at them. He felt he ought to be pleased. He could go home with their blessing, leaving them in safety for another generation at least. But he wasn't pleased; he felt that something had just gone horribly wrong. ("Yes, but,") he said again, ("the peace treaty, even if the one-eyes keep it, won't protect you for long. As soon as the witch-queen is dead, you'll be threatened again.")

("We will deal with that threat when it arises,") Avalanche said firmly.

("Yes, but—but—to Hades with it! *You won't be able to!* You probably can't defeat the one-eyes now, and in a generation, after conquering the Issedones, they'll be even more powerful! Then there are the Issedones to think of. I can't just leave them to be enslaved and eaten! And then there are the one-eyes themselves! If I refuse to lift the curse on them, why should I expect someone else twenty years from now to be more generous?")

("The future lies under the wings of the gods,") said Blizzard. ("What you have done is enough.")

("But it isn't!") Aristeas lashed his tail angrily. ("It wouldn't be enough if all that depended on it were the life of a single griffin cub! What decent person wouldn't give up a fortune to save a life? And there are thousands of lives at stake! After all, it's not as though I were being asked to die forever or suffer terrible torture. All I have to renounce is returning to one city. One can lose something like that, and go on living. I . . . No!") Blizzard and Avalanche looked as though they were about to speak, and he knew that he would have to act quickly. He clenched his talons and declared, ("I swear by Apollo, my master, by Zeus, by Artemis, by all the gods and goddesses, I swear the unbreakable oath by the river Styx, the boundary of the Underworld, that I here renounce all hope of ever returning to Proconnesus, my home. There. It's done, and can't be undone. Tomorrow morning I will do my utmost to break the curse.")

("I knew you'd never accept that offer and abandon us,") said Firegold proudly.

Aristeas flopped down and glared at his friend. ("Can't you say anything useful?") he asked. ("I'm starving; why don't you offer me something to eat?")

Firegold dashed off to fetch some food, and while Aristeas was eating, the First Ones and the assembled griffins decided how they would face the Arimaspian attack now.

("What do you need for the spell?") Blizzard asked Aristeas anxiously.

("My lyre,") he replied, and swallowed a strip of mutton. ("That, of course, means changing shape again. I'll do that after supper.")

("Must you?") asked Driftfeather.

("You think I can play a lyre like this?")

("No,") said Driftfeather sadly. Then, after a moment's hesitation, she said, ("I think we would all be pleased if you changed back again afterward.")

("I'll think about afterward afterward,") he said. ("Now I have to think about enchantments. The only thing I need, besides the lyre, is for the one-eyes to be able to hear it. That could be awkward. I imagine they'd shoot me on sight.")

("You told them you'd give them your answer to the peace proposals in the morning,") said Firegold. ("They'd have to let you near them to hear you.")

("They wouldn't wait for an answer if they had a good chance of killing him,") Avalanche said impatiently. ("But . . . Firegold has a point. We could arrange some kind of truce, somewhere where we could bombard them with stones if they tried anything treacherous.")

It was soon agreed. Aristeas left the First Ones debating locations and arguing about what to do if the one-eyes marched up the ravine during the night and went back to his room with Blizzard and Firegold. His tunic was still spread out on the floor, with the basin of water and the dish of coals. The water was dusty, and the fire had gone out. He sent the two griffins out to get fresh water and fire and sat down heavily. He felt immensely tired and depressed, and he didn't dare think about Proconnesus. He wished he could put off the shape changing until the next day, but he needed the night to recover before the spell he meant to work in the morning. At least changing back would be comparatively easy, since Blizzard had preserved the coal.

Comparatively easy still wasn't easy. The coal was reignited when Blizzard brought the fire, and Aristeas sang over it, and washed himself again in the water, and sang some more. By then he was so exhausted that he could barely lift the blazing coal and bring it to the full, sunlike brilliance it needed. But he told himself how much easier it was than it had been before and summoned the last effort. The coal consumed itself, dissolving into pure light on the great invocation, and then everything seemed to crumble at the edges and go black.

Out of the blackness he heard Firegold's anxious tones saying, ("Is he dead again?") and Blizzard replying, ("No, I think he's just fainted.") Water splashed his face, and he lifted a feeble hand to ward it off, then realized that it was a *hand* he'd lifted, not a claw. He sighed deeply.

("I'm all right,") he told the two griffins. ("Look after the fire and water, will you? I'm going straight to sleep.") And he did.

When he woke in the morning, the first things he looked at were his own hands. He held them in front of his face, opening and closing them and wriggling his fingers. He realized, rather to his own surprise, that he was going to miss his wings and feathers—but not his claws. Not in the least. Claws were useless for playing music, or writing, or mending, or even picking flowers. He felt much better, happier, and more peaceful about everything, now that he had hands again, and a voice.

Firegold wasn't in the cave, and he suspected that he himself was rather late getting up, but he didn't hurry. He went down to the hot springs and had a bath, then returned to his room and got dressed in his best tunic and cloak. He picked his lyre up and was tuning it lovingly when Firegold came in.

("You're awake at last!") exclaimed Firegold with relief. ("The one-eyes went through the ravine in the night. We did hurl more rocks at them, but between the darkness and their shields, we didn't do much damage. They're encamped beside the river now, on the slopes of the Shoulder of the World, about a hour and a half flight from the Fortress. We don't know how to arrange the truce with them, but the First Ones are sure you'll manage something.")

Aristeas grunted. ("After breakfast,") he said firmly.

After breakfast he took the parchment and pens out of

his saddlebags. ("Colaxis can read Greek,") he told the First Ones, who were watching in fascination. ("I'll write a letter to her, wrap it around a rock, and someone can drop it near her tent.") He spit on the little cake of dried ink, dipped the reed pen in it, and began writing, translating for the griffins as he went.

"Aristeas of Proconnesus to Colaxis, queen of the Arimaspians, sends greetings," he began. "Yesterday you proposed to me the terms on which you would make peace with the griffins. I wish to discuss the matter further. If you will meet with me, come yourself with"—("Do you think, a dozen supporters?")—"a dozen of your followers to"—("Did you decide on a good location? Where?")—"the foot of the waterfall of the White River. Your companions may bring clubs, but not bows, and the rest of your people must stay at least twice as far distant as a bow can shoot. I will meet you there at noon with a dozen companions. I swear by Apollo, my master, that I will work no enchantment to cause death or injury to any Arimaspian. In the god's name, farewell."

("Can you really say *that*?") asked Firegold. ("The swearing, I mean. I thought your god wouldn't let you lie.")

("I'm not lying!") Aristeas said indignantly. ("I'm just being misleading. Apollo can't object to that; he does it himself all the time.")

("Will your spell work to break the curse on the whole people, if there are only thirteen one-eyes who can hear it?") asked Nightfall.

("Of course!") said Aristeas in surprise, cleaning his pen. ("If it works, it wouldn't matter if only *one* one-eye heard it. A spell either works or doesn't.")

("*If* it works?") asked Avalanche, shocked. ("What do you mean, 'if'? It *will* work, won't it?")

Aristeas wrapped the letter around a lump of gold-veined quartz from the floor of the assembly hall and tied it with a piece of string. ("It should work,") he said. ("Abaris thought it would work. But how can anyone know for certain until it does? And Colaxis is a powerful magician herself, remember; she *might* be able to work a counterspell.")

("If you try it, and it doesn't work, the one-eyes at the meeting will kill you,") said Driftfeather.

("Yes,") agreed Aristeas. ("But if it doesn't work, we'll all die anyway, so what difference does it make? Who's going to carry the letter?")

Firegold took it in his beak. ("I'll drop it before the witch-queen's tent,") he promised.

("Make sure that you stay out of bowshot when you do!") Aristeas shouted after him as Firegold bounded off.

A couple of hours later Aristeas was waiting tensely at the meeting place. The White River, rushing down from the snows of the Shoulder of the World, crashed thunderously in a waterfall at his back, and its edges were bright with mountain flowers. Beside him stood all four First Ones, Firegold, and seven other griffins. Scouts had reported the movements of the Arimaspians: First that they were making for the meeting place; then that the main army had stopped and Colaxis was continuing on with her dozen companions. The letter's instructions were being followed, and the bows had been left behind.

There was a glint of gold down the slope, and then Colaxis appeared, followed by Hyrgis and eleven others. They all marched steadily without looking right or left and stopped only when they were a few feet away. Thirteen glaring red eyes fixed on Aristeas. After so much time and so much struggle, he and his enemies at last stood face-to-face.

The Two
Enchantments
===
11

"So," said Colaxis with contempt, "*this* is your true form."

Aristeas was uncomfortably aware that he looked very small and shabby beside her. His best tunic was pretty threadbare, and his head came only up to her shoulder. He scuffed a foot into the gravel and resisted the urge to stand tiptoe. "Greetings, Queen Colaxis," he said with pointed politeness.

She didn't take the hint. "You have decided to accept my terms for peace?" she demanded.

"We-ell," he said, "we've come to try to make a peace, yes." He knew he could not simply whisk out the lyre and start singing his spell. Her companions would certainly try to kill him if he did. He had to mislead them into allowing it. Colaxis would probably realize what was happening once the spell was under way, but if the enchantment were far enough along, she wouldn't be able to stop it.

"You know the terms. What more do you need?" demanded Hyrgis, shouldering his way up behind the queen.

Aristeas smiled. "I'm not from beyond the wind, Hyrgis, whatever you may think. I'm a Greek, and we Greeks don't believe what people tell us, just because they promise us it's true. I imagine we need to have guarantees of good faith on both sides. What guarantees are you willing to give?"

("What are you saying?") Avalanche wanted to know.

("That we don't trust each other,") replied Aristeas. Most of the Arimaspians flinched at the flicker-talk, but Hyrgis and Colaxis frowned as though they were working to understand it.

"We don't need to trust each other," said the queen. "We are both powerful magicians. We can use magic to guarantee this agreement. If you use your power to bind yourself to stay away, I'll use mine to bind myself to keep peace with the griffins."

Aristeas smiled again. This was going to be tricky; he had to give Colaxis the impression he'd agreed without actually doing so. "You said yourself, Queen," he began, "that it would benefit both of us if I accepted your proposal. The truth is, you were quite correct. I did learn a spell behind the wind that I could use on you, but it is costly. The price for working it is to renounce my heart's desire, which happens to be to return to my own city. So I suggest that I work my enchantment about the image of my home. How would you bind yourself to this agreement?"

"I have a potion that will be harmless to me if I keep my promise but poison if I break it," Colaxis said. She seemed to be relaxing a bit. "I will drink it—once you've bound yourself to your side of the bargain."

"So I go first?" asked Aristeas. "Very well. I can always work some other magic if you don't keep your word and swallow the brew." He strolled over to a large boulder, sat down on it, and unslung his lyre.

"One moment!" snarled Hyrgis, striding over to loom above Aristeas. "You swore by your god that you wouldn't work any enchantment at this meeting."

"I swore that I wouldn't work any enchantment to in-jure anyone," Aristeas corrected him. "And I won't. I swear it again now. But the queen expects me to bind my-self by magic. I couldn't very well do that without working magic, could I?"

Colaxis nodded to Hyrgis, who stepped back, and Aris-teas shifted his lyre against his shoulder and began to play.

He sang about Proconnesus: the white walls rising above the glittering sea, the flash of gulls' wings over the harbor, sunlight leaping astounded from the gilded statues in the marketplace, and the music of the townspeople's voices. He sang and began binding into the music the spell that Abaris had taught him. Never again, he sang, never again to return; many waters will flow between us, and the deep salt currents shift in the wine dark sea. Renouncing it before, he'd tried not to think of what he was losing, but now he bound his own grief in the strings of the lyre, and it seemed to him that his heart would break. He began to weep but sang on, and the spell deepened. The griffins leaned their heads against their wings in sorrow, and the Arimaspians stood motionless.

Colaxis stirred suddenly. "This is not a binding spell," she whispered. "This—this is . . . treachery!" She flung out her hands, pressing against the air. But the spell was strong now, and her scream came out faint and far away. Her followers stood gaping, unable to move. Aristeas played on. He was so wholly taken up by the magic now that he hardly knew who or where he was, and even the grief for Proconnesus seemed to belong to someone else.

Colaxis struggled to move and couldn't. She fumbled at her belt and found a jar of something. She flung it out-ward, over herself, over the nearest of her followers. There was a smell of blood. She curved her hands like claws and tore at the air as though she were ripping up invisible ropes. But beside her Hyrgis was the only one who started and looked around.

"He has betrayed us!" hissed Colaxis, leaning over to shake the captain of her guard. "He's working the spell from beyond the wind! Kill him! I'll give you all the protection I can!"

Hyrgis lifted one foot, heavily, as though he were uprooting it from the earth, and took a step toward Aristeas. Colaxis held her hands in the air before her as though she were trying to hold a door closed against a hurricane. Hyrgis took another step. He raised the long club-stick to his shoulder. Aristeas watched him coming, step by painful step. At the back of his mind, he knew that the Arimaspian would kill him with one blow, but he was so concentrated in the spell that he had no power left even to worry about it. Hyrgis took another step.

Then Firegold raised his head from his wing and stared at Hyrgis with dazed eyes. Perhaps, even in the power of the spell, he remembered Wing-shadow. His eyes began to clear, to take on a little of their usual fierce brilliance. He spread his wings. Hyrgis stepped nearer and raised the club.

Firegold leaped upward and glided through the air to strike against the Arimaspian's side. Hyrgis fell to his knees, dropping the club. He grabbed Firegold's neck just in time to hold the terrible beak away from his throat. Firegold kicked madly with his hind feet, raking the Arimaspian with his claws, ripping through the hide trousers and leaving long, bloody slashes; he clutched the powerful arms with his talons. Hyrgis gave a shout of pain that sounded dim and far away through the music, but he didn't let go. He began to twist Firegold's neck back, like a farmer killing a chicken. The griffin's wings beat frantically. Their force was so great that for a moment both struggling forms were lifted from the ground, and then both fell back to earth with a jolt. Hyrgis's hands loosened their grip for that moment, and Firegold lunged downward and tore at the Arimaspian's single eye with the arrow-sharp point of his beak. Hyrgis screamed and struck wildly at the griffin with all his strength, catching him on the shoulder and knocking him to the ground. The Arimaspian climbed to his knees, blood streaming from his eye, and fumbled blindly at the earth.

"No!" cried Colaxis. She stopped her struggle against the spell and staggered toward Hyrgis. She dropped on her knees beside him and caught his blood-covered arm.

"Queen!" panted Hyrgis, grasping her hand. "Queen, I can't see him, I can't kill him, I'm sorry . . ."

"Oh, my dearest, most loyal friend!" Colaxis cried, looking into his horribly torn face. "Oh, I shouldn't have asked it!"

Aristeas felt all at once as though something had given, that his enchantment had been building up like a lake behind a dam but now burst through the barrier and was crashing downward into the course it had always intended to take. Colaxis wept. The smooth hollows of her face grew damp, as though something were oozing through the skin, and then the slits of eyelids appeared, and tears poured from them. Colaxis opened her eyes to the dazzle of the sun and closed them again. She put both her arms about Hyrgis and leaned against him, sobbing in anguish.

Hyrgis, blinded in his one eye, suddenly began to cry from two. The other Arimaspians in the party began to sob so hard they couldn't stand and fell on their faces on the ground. The army waiting downstream collapsed as well, choking and beating the earth with their fists. And far away in its encampment in the shelter of the forest, the rest of the tribe wept, too. Babies that had howled and yelled, but never cried, were drenched with tears, and their mothers, who'd screamed and slapped, hugged them and sobbed into their soft hair. The whole Arimaspian people howled and wailed and screamed hysterically in floods of tears. Aristeas, dazed with it all, stopped playing. The meeting place was silent except for the steady roar of the waterfall and the sobs of the Arimaspians.

Firegold got stiffly to his feet. He rubbed his beak along his side where Hyrgis had hit him, then looked at Hyrgis and Colaxis, now weeping onto each other's shoulders. ("I suppose I can't kill him now,") he said.

("No,") agreed Aristeas. He felt so exhausted that he could barely hold his lyre. After a minute, though, he heaved himself to his feet, wavered over to Colaxis, and tapped her on the shoulder Hyrgis wasn't using. She looked up, still crying. Her face was wet and bright red, and her nose was running. Her new eyes were a brilliant blue—and swollen.

"Can we meet again tomorrow, Queen?" he asked her. "When you've had time to calm down?"

Colaxis only gasped. She buried her face in Hyrgis's shoulder again and kept crying. Hyrgis stroked her hair.

"Well"—Aristeas sighed—"I'll be here at noon tomorrow, anyway, if you want to talk. Same conditions as before. Farewell!" He stumbled to the sling that had been used to take him to the meeting place and dropped onto it. Firegold hurried over and wove one of the carrying straps across his own back.

("Are you all right to take it?") Aristeas asked. ("It looked as though Hyrgis hit you pretty hard.")

("I was just winded,") said Firegold. ("I'm all right.")

("If you say so. And thank you for saving my life. Again. I'm sorry I've been so . . . well, sharp with you lately.")

Firegold laughed. He leaned over and preened a lock of Aristeas's hair. ("I don't pay any attention to that anymore!") he said. ("You always cheep away with complaints like a three-day-old cub whose dinner's late, and you're worse when you're doing something noble. Everyone knows you don't mean it. I'm just glad I was able to stop that miserable earth-crawler in time.") He looked back at the collapsed Arimaspians. ("Are they going to be all right?")

("I should think so, once they've cried themselves sick,") said Aristeas. ("It can't be easy, having to shed the tears of a lifetime all at once. I don't imagine they're going to want to fight us or anyone else for some time. But we'll see them tomorrow and find out.")

The Arimaspians were at the meeting place early next day. Griffin scouts reported that Colaxis and twelve followers were making their way up to the waterfall when it was still a good hour before noon, and the griffin party had to hurry. As Aristeas was carried above the meeting place in his sling, he saw Colaxis and her friends standing in the middle of the only level patch, staring upward. The griffins had to lower him almost on top of them. And no sooner had the sling bumped the gravel than Colaxis rushed up and loomed over him, screaming, "You miserable treacherous liar!" She tried to slap him, and Aristeas, who hadn't even gotten to his feet, rolled over frantically to get out of her way. The griffins all squawked angrily and flapped their wings, but Colaxis paid no attention. "Look what you've done to us!" she wailed, and aimed a kick at Aristeas. Fortunately she'd burst into tears again, couldn't see properly, and missed.

"This is supposed to be a truce!" Aristeas exclaimed indignantly, scrambling out of the way and managing to stand up.

"It was supposed to be a truce yesterday!" replied Hyrgis, equally furious. "*And* you'd sworn not to injure us by enchantment—"

"Well? I didn't."

"You had my entire tribe on its knees yesterday!" screamed Colaxis. "The great Arimaspian nation, down on its knees, crying, like—like human babies!"

The griffins were bombarding Aristeas with anxious questions; he hushed them and tried to rush a translation as he continued. "We could have killed the lot of you," he told Colaxis sharply. "You were in no state to fight, and we could have destroyed you easily. But we didn't. The god I serve had freed you from a terrible curse, and we respected him and left you alone. You should think for a minute before you start kicking people." He glared at her, and she and Hyrgis glared back. Hyrgis's forehead was bandaged, but the queen's old eye was visible—and it didn't share the glare of her two new ones. In fact, it seemed to have glazed over, as though it were growing a skin. Glancing around at the other Arimaspians, Aristeas saw that their old eyes had glazed over, too, and some seemed to have grown smaller. They weren't flinching at the flicker-talk of the griffins, either. Perhaps they couldn't hear it anymore. The magical eyeholes were now unnecessary and had begun to close.

To his surprise, Aristeas also noticed Skylas, standing at the back of the party and looking younger with two baby blue eyes than he had with one red one. Hyrgis's former partner must have been pardoned in the outburst of tears. Skylas felt Aristeas's eyes on him and took a step nervously backward.

Aristeas looked back at Colaxis and found that she was standing next to Hyrgis, his arm around her, both pairs of blue eyes sparkling with anger. The sight of them so close gave him the courage to take a risk. "Do you want me to undo what I did yesterday?" he asked.

Colaxis gave a little gasp, and then there was a moment of absolute silence.

"Well?" asked Aristeas, looking around at the Arimaspians. "You, Hyrgis—Colaxis wept when she saw you injured yesterday, wept and caught you in her arms, where you wept, too. Do either of you really want never to weep again? And you there, hiding at the back, Skylas—do you want your queen to go back to being merciless?"

"But we were a strong people!" cried Colaxis. "I had such great ambitions for us! We were going to own all the gold of the griffins, and have the Issedones as our slaves! And now—now there's not a warrior who serves me who wants to fight this war. Even worse, I don't want to fight it myself! We've become weak, weak as humans! And soon the Issedones will overrun our lands, and what will become of us?"

"I don't think you're so weak that you'll be overrun by the Issedones," said Aristeas.

"Your Greek god prophesied that my power would end with my people's tears!" insisted Colaxis. "All the rest of that prophecy has come true. Only our ruin lies ahead."

"What did you actually ask Apollo?" said Aristeas.

"I asked whether I alone would rule the Arimaspians, and if so, for how long," replied the queen tearfully.

Aristeas smiled. That was an easy riddle to answer.

"And do you intend to go on ruling alone now?" he asked.
"Or are you going to take a partner?"

Colaxis looked at Hyrgis. "Well," she said, in surprised
hope, "I was thinking of ruling jointly—"

"Then the prophecy is fulfilled, without needing anybody's ruin," Aristeas declared with satisfaction.

"But without our old strength, how can we stop the
Issedones?" snarled Hyrgis. "They have horses. We don't.
They have bows, and they can make new ones whenever
they like. We have eighty magic bows, and the queen
doesn't think she can make any more; she said she doesn't
have the strength now to perform the sorcery."

"She doesn't have the cruelty, you mean," Aristeas answered. "But you don't need magic bows now. Hyrgis,
you're extraordinarily good at making things. You could
build a shield from the design you got from me, even with
your mind still locked under the curse. If you could build
a shield then, you'll certainly be able to build a bow now
that your mind is free. Study the design of the bows you
have, make new ones from ordinary wood, horn, and
sinew, and practice with them until you can shoot. Oh,
but, Skylas, bows belong in cases when not in use and
should be stored unstrung and dry. And keep your arm
out of the way of the string."

"Human bows always break for us," whined Skylas.

"Don't you understand?" Aristeas asked impatiently.
"The curse you were under prevented you from learning
anything new. And you'll find, I think, that you won't need
magic to tame horses now. You were unnatural creatures before, and no animal wanted to go near you, but now you're
human again it will be different. By the time the Issedones
even realize you've changed, you'll have bows and horses of
your own. Besides, though you say you're weak, look at

yourselves compared with . . . well, compared with me.
You're very large people and far from feeble. I don't think
you need to worry about the Issedones."

"Wait!" cried Hyrgis. "You say the—that what we
were before . . . prevented us from learning?"

"Of course! By Apollo, you can't learn without tears!
I don't think you can love properly, either, if you can't feel
anything but contempt for another's pain. You were in a
terrible state, though you didn't realize it. But already
you're starting to understand how much better off you are
now, and you don't want to go back to what you were.
Even a few days from now I think you'll bless me for deliv-
ering you."

There was another moment of silence, and then Hyrgis
looked at Colaxis. "What he's saying is true," he said.

Colaxis nodded. She lifted her griffin skull crown from
her head and tossed it into the middle of the watching First
Ones. "Very well," she said. Then she tossed back her hair
and began speaking slowly in flicker-talk, repeating her
words in the northern language for her Arimaspian listen-
ers. ("Griffins of the Fortress! I renounce my attack on
you and ask you to make peace. You know that we have
no heart to fight you now, and it seems we will be busy
learning new things for many years to come, too busy to
waste time making war on you.")

("We are willing to make peace,") said Avalanche,
speaking for them all. ("We ask only that you stay off our
land, and we'll stay off yours. You may take your army
and go.")

("Agreed,") said Colaxis. She looked around proudly,
then glared at Aristeas again. ("You owe much to your
magician, griffins. And perhaps my people owe something
to him as well. But I will *not* bless him for what he's done.

I am glad of the changes in our natures, I must confess it, but because of him, I have had to give up the plans for conquest that were the dearest desire of my heart, and I do not forgive him. I wish he—and all of you—were a thousand miles away, where I would never have to see you gloating over my humiliation!")

Aristeas's jaw dropped. "Do you really mean that?" he asked.

She gave him a look of loathing. "You expect me to thank you, do you?"

"Queen, having your thanks and blessings doesn't matter to me more than having the goodwill of a viper. But if you've really given up the dearest desire of your heart, and if you really want to send all of us to a place where you'll never see us again, well, it could be arranged."

When she understood that the griffins could all be sent beyond the wind, Colaxis at once agreed to help with the spell. Aristeas explained it to her, and it was arranged that they would try to perform it in three days' time.

As soon as he was back in the Fortress, Aristeas took Blizzard aside and, feeling unspeakably cruel, asked her to help, too.

("Of course,") said the old griffin. ("I was planning to as soon as you mentioned it.")

("But can you renounce your heart's desire?") Aristeas asked unhappily. ("Just like that? Don't you need to think about it first?")

("I renounced my heart's desire a long time ago, Excellent,") Blizzard replied gently. ("And it was something I could never get anyway.")

He looked at her, and she turned her head and looked back from a deep ruby eye. ("I wanted a mate and cubs,") she said. ("Not such an exceptional wish. But I was ugly, and a magician, and the young males never wanted me.")

("Ugly?") asked Aristeas in bewilderment.

("This horrible color.") Blizzard looked down at her snow white feathers. ("My eyes are horrible, too. I can't see with them very well, you know, not in sunlight, and so I was never a good hunter or a dashing scout or attractive in any way at all. The young males avoided me, and I grew older. And there came a time when I realized that either I could go on trying to find a mate and end up poisoned with bitterness, or I could let go and make the best of my life without the thing I most wanted. So I let go. I never swore any oath, as you did, and I would have been overjoyed if I had found a mate after all, but I think I renounced my heart's desire well enough to work the spell.")

Aristeas put an arm around her neck. ("Sweet-water Blizzard! I think you're a beautiful color!")

("Excellent, that's kind! Particularly from a young male as handsome as yourself—in your other form, that is. Driftfeather is in love with you, you know.")

("I thought she might be,") Aristeas said, letting go. ("She'd do better not to be.")

("She lost her mate five years ago, and you look a bit like him. He was killed by the one-eyes, and you've defeated them. I think she realizes in her heart that you don't want to look for a mate outside your own kind, but she can't help hoping. You wouldn't consider. . . ? We all hope you'll stay with us, since you can't go home.")

("Don't talk about that!") Aristeas said, getting to his feet. The mere mention of home hurt him. ("If I ever do give up the ties to my own kind, it will be so many years from now that it's not worth Driftfeather's time to wait for me. Why doesn't she think about Firegold instead? He's lost a mate, too, and I think he and Driftfeather would get on very well, once he gets over Wing-shadow.")

Blizzard gave him a look of deep amusement. ("I'll suggest it to her,") she said.

In the morning, in three days' time, they worked the spell that would set the Shoulder of the World beyond the wind. Colaxis stayed in the Arimaspian camp by the White River, brewing potions over a fire of spices, but Aristeas and Blizzard went to Sky-fire Mountain and stood on its flat top, now clear of snow and blackened by fresh lightning. The rest of the griffins watched from the surrounding slopes.

("I just hope Abaris has been watching, and things are ready on his side, too,") said Aristeas. He turned toward the sun and set his lyre against his shoulder.

("I am sure he has been watching,") said Blizzard tranquilly. ("He said he would be.") She spread her wings.

Out of thin air came a thread of music—not a lyre, this time, but a whole choir of voices singing, goldenly beautiful, but faint and far away. Blizzard's crest feathers stood up. ("He was watching,") she said happily. ("Listen! They've begun already.") She braced herself and flung into that faint music the single image of a golden light.

They performed the spell together: Aristeas playing the lyre, Blizzard singing her images, and Colaxis, back at the river, filling the air with clouds of fragrant smoke. The other voices faded in and out of the magic, and the sun rose higher in the sky, until it was standing directly above them. Then Blizzard leaped into the air and soared toward it, singing of the whole of the Shoulder of the World, its steep, stony peaks and blue glaciers, its waterfalls and rivers, its flocks of mountain sheep and its spring flowers. She turned in the air, singing, and Aristeas echoed her from the mountaintop, and the golden voices grew louder and clearer and stronger. All at once came a crack of wind like a hurricane, so powerful that Aristeas would have been blown from the mountaintop if the wind hadn't stopped as suddenly as it had begun. Then there was calm and a scent of jasmine and wild thyme, and the singing voices stopped.

Aristeas, who'd been knocked over by the wind, picked himself up, then picked up his lyre and checked carefully to see if it was broken. Blizzard glided down and landed beside him.

("Oh, Excellent!") she cried joyfully. ("Look! Look, it's beautiful!")

He looked out, and the stony blue valley he'd looked out over from the mountain that morning was gone. In its place was the land beyond the wind: rich green forests, meadows of flowers, pastures of tall grass, fields of grain, vineyards and orchards, birds, animals, and, gleaming at the mountain's foot, the town with the golden dome of Apollo's temple in its middle. And near the top of the slope from the city was a great crowd of people dressed in bright clothes. Abaris was standing in front of them.

"Welcome!" he shouted, waving both arms. Then, beaming, he added to Blizzard, ("Welcome, child of gold! Welcome to you and all your people! We are happier than we can say to see our neighbors once again!")

There was no doubting the enthusiasm with which the Hyperboreans welcomed the griffins. They raced up the mountain slopes, laughing and clapping, and enveloped Blizzard in a storm of goodwill. When the rest of the griffins flew over, they, too, found themselves surrounded by beaming humans and were soon all draped in flowers. Humans and griffins went together into the valley, where the Hyperboreans had prepared a feast of welcome. The griffins were offered goats and sheep to eat; the Hyperboreans had bread and cheeses, milk and little cakes of nuts and sesame seeds soaked in honey, and plenty of fruit and wine. Once the griffins had recovered from their first surprise and alarm at being so close to so many humans, they were as joyful as their new neighbors. They ate the sheep and goats and then tried human food, and there was music and singing and eating and drinking for the rest of the day. At one point Aristeas noticed the two boys who'd first welcomed him. They were playing with a golden ball, tossing it from one to another, while a half-grown griffin cub tried to catch it in midair. The game ended when the griffin crashed into one of the boys, and all three rolled over on the ground shouting or flickering laughter.

Toward evening the Hyperboreans began to dance in a great circle, and at this most of the griffins leaped into the air and began to dance as well, turning and swooping in the sky of their new home. Aristeas noticed that Firegold was dancing with Driftfeather, and he smiled.

Aristeas himself could not dance. He had eaten and drunk and sung with the rest, and enjoyed the bread and wine, but not as much as he'd expected. Even the sound of everyone praising him, normally so delicious, didn't please him. He kept thinking of Proconnesus, and his heart ached for it. As the stars came out, he left the singing and danc- ing crowds and walked slowly into the empty town. The temple of Apollo was dark and silent, and he sat down on the steps outside it and began to pick out a very fiddly, complicated sort of tune on the lyre.

"You miss your home?" asked a deep, musical voice.

He glanced around. It was dark, and he couldn't see clearly, but he could just make out a tall, fair-haired shape standing in the porch of the temple behind him. Abaris, he thought. He picked out a few more notes on the lyre. "Yes," he admitted.

The other came over and sat down beside him. "Do you know what would have happened if you had accepted Colaxis's offer and gone home to Proconnesus?" he asked.

"The griffins would all have been dead within a generation," said Aristeas flatly. "I know, what I gave up was worth it."

"Actually, they wouldn't have been dead within a generation," replied the other. "The Fortress would have been sacked about thirty years from now, but there would have been a few isolated griffin families living in the mountains for a couple of centuries afterward until they all died out. But I actually meant what would have happened to you?"

Aristeas snorted. "How could I know? But I suppose you're going to tell me."

"Yes. When you got back, your father would have been overjoyed to see you. He would instantly have tried to get a place for you on the city council. Many of your fellow citizens wouldn't have been eager to elect you; to them, you wouldn't have been just the son of a notorious aristocrat but also a magician, the man who dropped dead in a wool shop and disappeared for seven years. They'd all be afraid you'd cast spells on them or disappear again. However, your fame and your father's influence would be enough to make them elect you, though in the process, you'd make enemies. Then your father would choose you a wife—Agathon's daughter Glykis."

"Glykis?" asked Aristeas in surprise. "You mean my friend Leontes's little sister, the fat girl? How do you know about her?"

"The fat girl," agreed the other. "Now even fatter. Sweet-natured but unsure of herself. She'd be terrified of you, and she'd ask your permission to do anything, even to clean the kitchen. You'd lose your temper and shout at her, and then she'd be even more terrified. You'd be ashamed of yourself but more and more unpleasant and sarcastic with her, and the marriage would make both of you miserable. To escape from it, you'd throw yourself into the business of the council, where you'd find your enemies more offensive every day. Your magic would start slipping away from you, and you'd worry about that and work even harder at the council. You wouldn't compose any poetry because you'd be too busy and too anxious for it. You'd join your father and some of his friends in a plot to make the system of government more aristocratic—and it would be discovered. And finally you'd die, the victim of a political assassination, three years after returning to Proconnesus."

Aristeas stared. A shaft of moonlight had crept into the porch, and he saw now that the man he was speaking to was not Abaris. Tall, like him, and fair-haired, but dressed in a Greek tunic and carrying on his back a bowcase and a lyre. Aristeas got to his feet, still staring. "How do you know these things?" he asked faintly.

"I know these things," the other replied confidently. "That's why everyone sends to Delphi to ask me."

Aristeas wanted to run, or burst into tears, or throw himself flat on the ground. "My lord Apollo!" he gasped. "I—I—I'm sorry . . ."

"Whatever for?" asked the god.

"I—I didn't—I haven't . . . I've cursed you and been angry and arrogant."

Apollo laughed. "As Firegold says, you cheep complaints like a three-day-old cub whose dinner's late. But I don't pay any more attention to it than he does. You've done everything I wanted you to do. Oh, it's true, you're a conceited idiot at times, but there are worse faults, and not many men would sacrifice their heart's desire for the safety of another race." He stood up, and rested a hand on Aristeas's shoulder. "I'm pleased with you," he said.

"But—but," Aristeas stammered in confusion, "is this real? Do you really look like this?"

"You Greeks!" said Apollo. "You and your questions! Chatter, chatter, chatter, is this possible, why is it, how can it be, what is the universe made from, what is the nature of the soul! You Ionians would take the whole cosmos to bits to examine it, if you could. You know I'm real already. Don't worry about the rest."

"But—but . . . what am I to do now?"

"Do you want me to give you another task *immediately*?" asked Apollo. "I know you love travel and adventure, for all your complaints about it, but I thought you might want to rest for a while first. Eat bread, and sleep in a bed in a proper bedroom with floors. In a few years, when you're bored with doing nothing, there are plenty of places I could send you if you really want to go."

Aristeas stared at him. "Are you laughing at me?" he asked.

Apollo tossed his head back and laughed. "Oh, Aristeas!" he exclaimed affectionately. "Would I do that?"

And then he was gone, and Aristeas was left smiling into the moonlight, listening to the echo of the god's laughter.

Author's Note

There really was a Greek poet called Aristeas of Proconnesus. He was born in the seventh century B.C. on the island that's now called Marmara, in the Sea of Marmara, which lies between the Black Sea and the Mediterranean. You can't read his poem on the Arimaspians because it was lost long ago, but we know he existed because the Greek historian Herodotus wrote about him. Herodotus had read Aristeas's poem to find out about the northeastern part of the world. Aristeas was one of the few Greeks who ever journeyed far in that direction and came back to write about it.

It's in Herodotus's *Histories* that you can read about the Scythians and about the Issedones and the werewolf Neuroi and the rest, who lived in southern Russia and the Ukraine through to Siberia before the time of Christ. Modern historians and archaeologists are very fond of Herodotus because his descriptions of these people seem to be pretty accurate wherever they can be checked by archaeology. Herodotus also repeats what the real Aristeas said about griffins, Arimaspians, and Hyperboreans, though he says that Aristeas didn't claim to have seen these people himself. ("Personally, however," says Herodotus, "I refuse to believe in one-eyed men who in other respects are like the rest of us"—Her. III:116.) The griffins' mountains are probably the Altai range in southwestern Siberia, where there actually is quite a lot of gold. I'm afraid, however, that my own descriptions of Arimaspians and griffins will not be confirmed by archaeology. I made them up to please my sons, and I hope they've pleased you as well.

That Aristeas is supposed to have been a magician, though, is not something I invented. It's Herodotus who tells the story about Aristeas's dropping dead in a shop in Proconnesus and then disappearing for seven years, reappearing, composing his poem, and vanishing again. He goes on:

> I will add something which I know happened to the people of Metapontum in Italy two hundred and forty years (as I found by computation) after the second disappearance of Aristeas. There the story goes that Aristeas appeared and told them to erect an altar to Apollo, with a statue beside it bearing the name of Aristeas of Proconnesus; then, after explaining that they were the only people in Italy whom Apollo had visited, and that he himself on the occasion of his visit had accompanied the god in the form of a raven, he vanished. The Metapontines sent to Delphi to ask the oracle what the apparition signified, and were advised that they had better do what it recommended. This advice they took, with the result that in the marketsquare of the town a statue inscribed with the name of Aristeas stands today by the side of the image of Apollo, surrounded by myrtle bushes.
>
> HERODOTUS, *Histories*, Book IV, Chapter 16
> translated by de Selincourt

What do you suppose Aristeas was *doing* visiting a Greek city in southern Italy in the shape of a raven with a god for company?

I only need to add that the poem about the shield is my own translation of one by another seventh-century Ionian Greek, Archilochos of Paros.

A modern classical scholar who has written a very

learned book on Aristeas concludes it so charmingly that I can do no better than repeat him:

> The reputation of the old wizard of Proconnesus . . . may still linger somewhere today, connected as ever with strange things, for the ship which in 1938 fished up a living coelacanth, as it were from the Mesozoic era, was called *Aristea*.
>
> J. D. P. Bolton
> *Aristeas of Proconnesus*
> (Oxford, 1962)